THE GREAT GOOD THING

THE GREAT GOOD THING

A novel by Roderick Townley

SCHOLASTIC INC.

New York Toronto London Auckland Sydney
Mexico City New Delhi Hong Kong Buenos Aires

ISBN 0-439-39784-7

Copyright © 2001 by Roderick Townley.
All rights reserved. Published by Scholastic Inc.,
557 Broadway, New York, NY 10012, by arrangement with
Atheneum Books for Young Readers, an imprint of Simon &
Schuster Children's Publishing Division. SCHOLASTIC and
associated logos are trademarks and/or registered trademarks
of Scholastic Inc.

12 11 10 9 8 7 6 5 4 3   2 3 4 5 6 7/0

Printed in the U.S.A.   01

First Scholastic printing, April 2002

Book design by Ann Bobco
The text of this book is set in Granjon.

acknowledgments

I'm grateful to the Kansas Arts Commission and the National Endowment for the Arts for the gift of time in the form of an Individual Artist Fellowship for Fiction. Thanks also to Wyatt Townley, who asked me to tell her a bedtime story, then made me write it down; to Grace Townley for ideas on making it better; to Zoey Howe for urging herfather to hurry up and read the thing; to James Howe for listening to his daughter and helping the book on its way; to Amy Berkower for knowing just where to send it; to Richard Jackson for exceptional editing; and finally, to the girl with the dark blue eyes.

—R. T.

For Wyatt and Grace

contents
෴

Part One

SYLVIE LOOKS UP

chapter one

Sylvie had an amazing life, but she didn't get to live it very often. What good were potions and disguises if no one came along to scare you or save you or kiss you behind the waterfall? Week after week nothing changed. A year went by. The sparkles on Sylvie's dress began to fade, and a fine dust coated the leaves, turning the green woods gray.

Once in a while, it looked as though something might happen. The ground trembled slightly, then nothing more. People got used to these disturbances. King Walther scarcely noticed. He sat about playing cards with the goatherd. Even the wolves stopped lurking and just lay in the heat, panting like house dogs. It got so that one day

Sylvie sat down on a stone at the edge of the lake and wept.

"Come on," she whispered fiercely. "Come on! Something happen!"

At that moment, a fan of light began opening in a corner of the sky, sending flashes of color across the water. Sylvie wiped her eyes as the woods brightened. A breeze flew through the treetops, knocking against branches as it went.

"*Rawwwwk!* Reader! Reader!" cried an orange bird, bursting into the air.

"Booook open!" groaned a bullfrog. "Ooopen! Boook open!"

Sylvie sprang to her feet, excitement and fear catching in her throat. How far had she wandered? A distant trumpet sounded, and the forest echoed with clumping hooves, flapping wings, shouting knights, fluttering dowagers, all racing to get to their places.

Sylvie had the farthest to go—all the way to page 3—but she knew the shortcuts between descriptions and arrived, hot-cheeked, just as a shadow moved over the land and the face of an enormous child peered down on her.

She didn't care for the look on that face—it was a boy with a pouty lip—but she could spare him no more than a glance. Her dialogue began right away.

"Father," she said, "I cannot marry Prince Riggeloff."

Her father was breathing hard. He'd had to run in heavy robes from page 13. "Not marry Riggeloff?" cried the king. Sweat stood on his pasty brow. "For heaven's sake, child, he is handsome, rich . . ."

"Kind, brave," continued Princess Sylvie. "Yes, I am aware of his qualities."

"He has everything."

"So have I," the girl replied, dodging around an illustration.

"You don't have a husband."

"Nor want one. I don't want *anything*," she said, her green eyes flashing, "except—"

But Sylvie, who had arrived at the top of page

3

4, never got to say what it was she wanted. A gob of strawberry jam hurtled from the sky and landed with a *splot*, just two words in front of her, spattering her blue shoes. She looked up. The boy was biting into a peanut butter sandwich. He wasn't even listening!

"Dumb story," he humphed and, without bothering to wipe away the jam, he slammed the book shut and tossed it.... Well, Sylvie could only *imagine* that he tossed it, for she found herself and King Walther and all the courtiers spinning around, then bumping to a stop at a backward angle. They waited in darkness, but the boy did not reappear.

"Watch out!" came the high, scratchy voice of Pingree the Jester. "Get off of me, you lunk!"

"Sorry," sounded the basso voice of the king's chief councillor.

"If only you had as much wit as you have width!"

The backup lights buzzed and flickered and came on. The sky, a storybook blue, appeared through the castle window, and the ladies-in-waiting picked themselves off the floor and righted their chairs.

The king was rubbing his hip. "Are you all right, child?"

"I suppose so," said Sylvie.

"One of these days we'll get a real Reader."

She gave him a doubtful look.

"We used to have them, lots of them," he said.

"Father, we never had *lots* of Readers."

"Well, we had good ones. They paid attention."

Sylvie mumbled something.

"What was that, dear?"

"Nothing."

"Don't say that. This is a book. We have to say everything."

"I said, maybe they found something better to do than read our silly story."

Queen Emmeline had been gazing critically in a mirror, poking at her ruined hairdo. "Sylvie," she said in her warning voice.

"Never mind," said the king. "She knows it isn't true. The sun shines. Readers read."

5

Sylvie had heard all that before. It didn't make her feel any better.

"We have a big responsibility," the king went on.

"I know."

"If it weren't for us —"

"I know!" The princess smoothed the folds of her skirt and started toward the edge of the page. "I think I'll take a nap, if nobody minds."

Queen Emmeline glided up to her husband and laid her hand on his arm as Sylvie disappeared in the direction of page 6.

She found a comfy spot on the left-hand margin beside the seventh paragraph and rested her head on "grandiloquent," the largest adjective in sight. As her head sank into the stuffing, the earlier thought returned: What if Readers really did have other lives, lives that had nothing to do with her world? The idea went against everything she'd been taught.

The sun shines. Readers read. She nestled down and yawned. Soon her breathing softened as she drifted into a dream about Chapter Four, in which she sets out on her quest to regain the stolen treasure. As always, the dream went pretty much the way the story was written. Following the thieves' trail, she rode her donkey into the forest. In a clearing she came across a great tortoise — ten feet across — which local peasant boys had somehow overturned and left to die. Dark birds stared down from the trees. Sylvie tried to help, but the tortoise was too heavy. She used a long pole as a lever and tied a length of rope to her donkey. With her pushing and the donkey tugging, the tortoise finally thumped over onto its feet. It looked at her several long seconds with its great reptilian eyes, then disappeared in the undergrowth.

Sylvie traveled on. In the afternoon heat, she heard a high clicking sound and the beating of wings. Ahead, in a thornbush, a large snowy owl struggled. The more desperately it beat its wings, the deeper the thorns pierced its body. Bright red

7

lines worked their way down the white feathers. Then Sylvie realized (as she always realized at this point in the story) that the bird's *eyes* were white, too. It was blind!

"Shh," Sylvie said in a soft voice. "Hush, little one."

The owl grew calmer, and Sylvie was able to stroke its back. She held the quivering bird and gently pulled away the thorns. With a cry the owl exploded into the air, circled her once, and flew north.

At last, her petticoats hopelessly dusty, Sylvie arrived at the cliffs overlooking the Mere of Remind. The waters of the Mere were usually calm, but now something was churning up waves close to the shore. An enormous fish of some kind, she thought, trapped by the receding tide. She hurried down to the water.

"There, there, fish," she said, extending her hand over the thrashing waves. "If you will calm down, I will help you." She reached below the surface and felt the scaly back of a great sea creature.

She waded in, stroking the fish all the while. It blended so perfectly with the water, it seemed invisible. "Come," she said. She bumped into the dorsal fin and gently pulled on it, guiding the fish to a place where it could wriggle over a sandbar and escape.

"Now!" she cried. The creature heaved itself up, and Sylvie pushed with all her strength while sand flew everywhere. In that moment, catching the last sunlight, the fish's sand-covered body was briefly visible. "Why, you're as big as a drawing room!" Sylvie gasped. Then it slammed back in the water and was gone.

She watched the flashing waves grow brighter and brighter, till she had to shield her eyes. The distant cliffs were turning transparent. What was happening? Then came the sound of screaming birds, and a low grumbling.

"Booook open! Ooooopen!"

9

Sylvie woke from her dream in a panic. The page was flooded with light. She started running, already late. A face was peering down into the royal chamber, where the king was chewing on the end of his mustache and looking around anxiously.

"Father-I-cannot-marry-Prince-Riggeloff!" Sylvie gasped as she raced out onto the page.

"Not marry Riggeloff?" King Walther beamed, relieved to see her back in place. Then he caught himself and harrumphed. "For heaven's sake, child, he is handsome, rich . . ."

Sylvie had to lean against the wall to catch her breath. Her hand rested on a suit of armor. "Kind, brave, yes, I . . ." The armor started to scrape along the wall. "Yes, I . . ."—she made a grab for it and missed—"know!" she cried as the armor, with a stupendous crash, landed on the stone floor. "No! No!"

One of the ladies-in-waiting fainted dead away. Somewhere someone started giggling.

"He has—he has," started the king. He cast a

worried glance at the large woman lying on the floor.

The giggling grew louder.

"Everything, yes I know," Sylvie said. "So do I."

"And so do I!" her father exclaimed.

"Of course you do!" cried Sylvie. "You're the king!"

"Where am I?" The lady-in-waiting, a round woman in a bulging ball gown, was struggling onto her elbow.

Pingree the Jester hid his face in his pointed hat.

"And you're the princess!" shouted the king to Sylvie. He put his hand to his brow. "What am I saying?"

The laughter grew louder. Sylvie glanced up, just for a second, and saw a huge face in the sky. A girl, she realized, one she hadn't seen before. "Ah-ha-ha-ha!" the girl boomed out, gripping the sides of the book till the castle shook.

The laughter died away. The new Reader had turned the page and found 4 and 5 stuck together. Sylvie forgot the number one rule of all storybook characters: *Never look at the Reader.* It was a rule she had broken before, but this time she just stared up at the Reader, a plain-looking girl a bit younger than herself, with short brown curls and a mouth too wide for her face. She was prying the pages apart.

"That Ricky!" the girl cried. Then she closed the book and left the courtiers in darkness.

"Oh!" King Walther sighed in despair.

"Disaster!" the jester groaned, flicking dust from his jingling cap.

"She may come back," said the queen.

Sylvie and her father helped pull the lady-in-waiting to her feet as the backup lights sputtered and blinked on. No one spoke, or even looked at each other. Two disappointments in one day, after years of sitting on an undusted shelf. It was too much!

chapter two

One of the younger thieves stepped over to Sylvie. "Are you all right, Your Highness?"

She looked up in surprise. "Oh hello, Thomas."

He pulled a linen handkerchief from his sleeve.

"What's that for?"

"You seem to be crying, Your Highness."

"I am not crying!"

"Of course not."

"And save the 'Your Highness' for my mother."

Thomas bowed his head. "I'm sorry to have offended you."

Now Sylvie really did lose patience. "Thomas, you're a thief! A thief! That's the way you were conceived. Stop acting like a courtier!" Nonetheless, she did dab at the corner of her eye with the handkerchief. "Sorry," she said in a quieter voice. "It's not your fault."

"It probably is. A thief is usually at fault."

"Not this time, I messed up that scene all by myself."

"Yes, Your Highness."

Sylvie gave him a sharp look. "Thomas," she said, shaking her head, "why don't you go off and steal something?"

The servants were setting the armor against the wall when they noticed the breastplate growing brighter, then blindingly bright.

"Hey!" Pingree cried, jumping up on a chair. "They're doing it again!"

"Everyone to your places!" King Walther shouted as the roof lifted away and the girl's face reappeared above them. Her tongue was lodged in the corner of her mouth as she reached down with an enormous rag. Everyone dove for cover, the jester closing himself inside parentheses, Queen Emmeline wedging herself into a dependent clause, and Sylvie racing to the Dedication page, where she disappeared among a dozen names, including the author's pets and several friends without whose help this book could not have been written.

The Reader wiped carefully at the strawberry jam. She squinted, licked a corner of the rag, and rubbed at the place again. It was not a pleasant sight.

That's the last time I walk through *that* sentence! thought Sylvie.

The Reader blew on the page, then began looking for where she'd left off. That took a while. It always takes Readers time when the characters aren't where they belong. Sylvie raced breathlessly through the undergrowth of description, emerging on page 3 just in time to blurt: "But I don't want *anything*, except—"

The king, confident of his lines now, made a show of anger: "Except what, for heaven's sake? Speak!"

15

"Tell us, darling," said Queen Emmeline, gliding across the page in a shushing of silks. Her hair, Sylvie noticed, was perfect.

Sylvie blushed, but stood her ground. "I'm sorry. I can't marry anyone."

"What do you mean?" The queen's voice had an edge.

"I have everything, but I have done nothing. Before I marry, I must do one Great Good Thing."

"What *sort* of thing?" The queen's eyes narrowed.

"Don't you think marrying Prince Riggeloff is doing a great thing?" said the king.

"No," said Princess Sylvie. "Even if I trusted him, which I don't, marrying is what I do *after* I do the Great Good Thing."

"But this is absurd!" the queen exclaimed hotly. "You're twelve years old! It's time to think of marriage, not—adventure!"

The princess could feel the cool shadow of the Reader overhead and hear her breathing. Storybook characters live for the sound of Readers breathing, especially as it softens and settles like the breath of dreamers. It gives the characters courage to go on through the most difficult plot twists. This Reader's breathing continued to accompany Sylvie right to the end of the book. It quieted in Chapter Three, when Prince Riggeloff, embittered by the princess's refusal and desperate for a rich bride, sent his band of retainers and hired ruffians to rob the castle. The breath caught in the Reader's throat when the horrid man in the Cave of Diamonds demanded that Sylvie kiss the open wound on his forehead. The breath came and went, sighing, halting with fear, as she rescued the blind owl from the thorn-bush, and later as a great fish saved her from drowning by swallowing her, its body transparent as glass. Finally there was the short intake of breath, followed by a sigh, as Riggeloff met his horrible end, and the ancient Keeper of the Cave turned into a young prince.

Then the most extraordinary thing happened.

The Reader murmured the final words to herself, gave a little hum, and turned to the front again. She flipped past the Acknowledgments and Contents and started over! Such a thing had not happened since the very earliest days, when a certain young person, a girl with dark blue eyes, used to peer down into the kingdom almost constantly. That was many years ago, a strangely exciting time. The girl would read the words over and over in a sort of whisper, surprised and pleased as if they were her own. You didn't find Readers like that nowadays.

The main characters were bone tired after their first full-length performance in years, but Sylvie rallied them by throwing herself back into her role. The others responded and soon were giving their best performance ever.

"Father," she said, and paused. There was dignity in the way she carried herself, her chin lifted, her voice soft but clear. "I cannot marry Prince Riggeloff."

King Walther seemed stunned. "Not marry Riggeloff?" He walked to the window, considering her words, then turned to face her. "For heaven's sake, child! He is handsome, rich . . ."

She lowered her head. "Kind, brave," she said, "yes, I am aware of his qualities."

"He has everything!"

The girl flashed him a look. "So have I!"

"You don't have a *husband!*"

"What?" came a voice from above. "What's going on?"

Sylvie glanced around at the ladies-in-waiting, imagining that one of them had forgotten when to come in. They were always forgetting their entrances.

"Where's the suit of armor?" cried the same echoey voice. Suddenly, everything was thrown on its side as the Reader began riffling through the pages.

"Where's the funny part?" They heard the voice somewhere above them as the cascading

19

pages tossed them about. The Reader started opening and reading at random, trying to find the parts that had made her laugh, but she could make no sense of what she read because the characters barely had time to arrive before she flipped to another page.

"Whatcha looking for, Claire?" came a boy's voice out of heaven.

The Reader stopped turning pages and held the book open against her. "I was trying to find something."

"You *like* that book? Princesses and all that stuff?"

Sylvie poked her head from a thicket of description.

"So what?"

"Why don't you read something real, like volcanoes? Do you know anything about volcanoes?"

"I know lots of things."

"Like what?"

"I know how to read a book without slopping food on it."

20

"Phoo."

"Anyway, what's so real about those treasure maps of yours?" said the girl.

"There really is treasure. I read about it in a magazine. They sent out this expedition."

The girl laughed. "I don't think they'd use your maps. You make them up and burn them around the edges to make them look old."

"So?"

"So they aren't any realer than my book."

"You should try it, just around the edges. It looks neat."

"Are you crazy? What's this thing you've got with matches?"

"What thing?"

"If Mom ever found out . . ."

"I just like to make things look old. Like parchment. Your book would look really neat."

"You want to burn the edges of my book?"

"It isn't your book, anyway."

"It is so. Grandma gave it to me before she went into the hospital the first time."

21

"You got any witnesses?"

"She gave it to me, Ricky. She called me into her room and gave it to me."

"Let me see."

"Keep your sticky fingers away!"

The voices were cut off as the book snapped shut. Darkness closed over castle and forest. Slowly, Sylvie stood. "Are you there, Father?" she called softly. The backup lights had not yet come on.

"Over here," came his distant voice. "Page 23, I think."

"Is Mother all right?"

"I wish Readers would be more careful. Her dress is ruined."

"Her dress is messed, the Reader's a pest, and that's no jest." In the darkness, Pingree's voice sounded like a scratch on black slate.

There was the usual buzzing sound for the backup lights, but only some of them came on. The king called for the mechanic.

"I'll be glad to fix it, sir."

"No, Thomas," said the king. "You're a thief, remember?"

"Yes, sir."

"Thieves aren't helpful."

"No, sir."

"Where would we be if we all started playing parts that weren't written for us?"

"I'm sure I don't know, sir."

"Sylvie, is it beginning to get lighter in here?"

"You're right, Father!"

"We're not ready!"

"Hurry!"

The book flew open, pages flittering, and stopped at the half-page illustration on page 35, the one with Sylvie riding inside the invisible fish to the bottom of the Mere of Remind. Sylvie raced over and slipped into the picture. It was one of her favorite scenes, and she wasn't surprised the Reader had returned to it. What did surprise her was the huge tear that fell onto the page like a great, warm jellyfish. She looked up. The Reader's nose was red, and her underlip quivered.

Then she moved away and Sylvie could see only the ceiling of a room and a lighting fixture. Either *read* the book or *close* the book! she thought.

For several minutes the ceiling light stared down at them like an unforgiving sun. Finally there was movement in the room, and the girl returned. At least her brown curls appeared along the eastern horizon. What was she *doing?*

The book remained open. Just open. Sylvie waited a long time, listening to distant breathing. The fish twitched its tail expectantly.

"Excuse me," Sylvie said, climbing out of the fish's mouth onto a rock. She still couldn't see, so she clambered up the cliff near the top of the page. The woods lay to the east, as always, but beyond it there seemed to be more woods, a different woods. The sound of breathing grew soft and regular, and Sylvie realized the girl had fallen asleep.

"Sylvie, what are you doing?" It was her mother's voice from the page after next.

24

"Just looking around. Did you ever notice that forest over there?"

"You get right back in that fish, young lady! Do you realize the book is open?"

"Just a minute."

She was sure the other forest hadn't been there before. "I'll be right back." She hurried along the cliff and down a sloping path into the woods. An orange bird screamed at her: "Reader! *Rawwwk!*"

"Oh, hush!" Sylvie said irritably.

Up ahead, the cool woods she loved changed into a different place altogether. The oaks and beech trees of her father's kingdom gave way to ragged palms and plants with rubbery leaves. Sylvie knew she shouldn't go farther. If it was against the rules just to look at the Reader once in a while, she could imagine what her parents would say about leaving the kingdom!

Yet right before her lay a world strangely different from the orderly land she lived in. Only a

25

narrow strip of white, like a margin, marked the borderline, and a tropical breeze blew across it from the other side, carrying the heavy smells of flowers. Her obedience to her parents made her hesitate. They were probably wondering where she was right now. Still, when had *any* character had the chance to explore a Reader's dream? It was irresistible!

She took a deep breath. "Here goes," she whispered, and stepped across.

chapter three

Suddenly, instead of the chirr of squirrels, big ring-tailed monkeys screeched from the forest canopy. A bee the size of a mitten whizzed past her head and disappeared in the blurred light.

Sylvie followed a muddy path into the jungle. She knew she should turn back, and she *would;* but while she was here she might as well see what was what. A great root, muscular as an anaconda, sent her sprawling. She looked at herself. Her parents kept making her promise not to get her clothes dirty, and she always came home a mess. It wasn't her fault. Did they expect her to explore jungles in a party dress?

They didn't expect her to explore jungles at all. And her hair, long and brown, difficult to control at any time, had worked itself free of the combs. She couldn't worry about that now. The smell of smoke struck her as she hurried on. At last she came to a clearing. Huts of woven swamp grass stood in a semicircle, and two of them were ablaze, smoke twisting into the sky. A distant voice called out, but she could see no one. She went on, leaving the huts behind. The path grew boggier, deepening into a ribbon of mud that soaked her shoes. Sylvie heard sloshing footsteps ahead, coming toward her, and stopped, undecided whether to run or stay. I'm not sure I like this story, she thought.

Around the bend, a girl a little younger than herself came struggling through the mud. She was dressed like a peasant, but not like any peasant in Sylvie's book. Her narrow trousers were made of a faded denim material, and her short-sleeved shirt bore a strange message in curling letters. Sylvie had never seen costumes with words on them before.

The girl looked up, fear in her eyes and a smear of mud on her cheek. "Princess Sylvie!" she cried.

Sylvie recognized her round face at once. "You're the new Reader!"

"Help me! They've taken my grandma!"

"Who has?"

"The thieves. You know. The thieves!"

"Riggeloff's thieves?" said Sylvie in disbelief.

The girl reached out and grabbed Sylvie's hand to pull herself along through the mud. Distant shouts and crashes filled the air.

"I don't know what to do," said Sylvie. "This is not my story."

"Hide me!"

They happened to be under a large tree. Sticky droplets fell from the tips of sweaty leaves. "Here!" Sylvie cried, pulling herself onto a low branch.

"I can't do that!"

29

Sylvie hopped down again. "Quick!" she said, interlocking her hands. "I'll give you a lift up."

The girl hesitated. Her soft, unmuscled body was not used to this sort of thing. Finally she lifted her muddy foot to Sylvie's hands. Once the girl was up, Sylvie followed like a monkey. Together they climbed out onto a fat branch overhanging the path just as a group of men and hollering dogs burst into view.

"Who are those people?" whispered Sylvie.

But the Reader wasn't listening. She held her hand over her mouth. When the men were gone, the girls looked at each other.

"What is it?" said Sylvie.

"Ricky," she whispered.

"The boy with the jam?"

She nodded. "He was the one carrying the torch and the treasure map."

Sylvie shook her head admiringly. "You've sure got a great story. How does it turn out?"

"What do you mean?"

"Does your brother get swallowed by a snake

or something?" Sylvie looked at the girl's puzzled face. "You mean you don't *know* how your own story turns out?"

The girl shook her head. "All I knew was that you'd save me."

"But I'm not even supposed to be here."

"You do Great Good Things. I haven't even done little good things. I couldn't keep them from taking my grandmother."

A huge vermilion butterfly flapped by, stirring the leaves.

Sylvie looked at the girl. She had a good face, open. Although far from pretty, the girl looked nicer than before, and Sylvie realized she'd only seen her from below. She'd thought all Readers had big noses and fat chins, but probably it was the angle. "Your name is Claire?" she said.

"You know me?"

"I heard you talking with your brother. Did he really kidnap your grandmother?"

"Oh, I don't know. He's only a kid." She started

31

crying. "You have to help me! You fooled the thieves before."

"I have to get back," Sylvie said. The king and queen were probably frantic by now.

"But what's going to happen to me?" Claire seemed on the verge of wailing.

"I wouldn't worry about that. Stories always turn out right in the end."

"Not for me!"

Sylvie was amazed at the thought. "My story does. Every time."

"Please stay!"

Sylvie squeezed Claire's hand. "I'd love to. To tell the truth, Prince Riggeloff sometimes gets on my nerves. It would be fun to see what another story's like."

"Well, then?"

"I can't."

"But if you're bored with Riggeloff . . ."

"No, no." She looked around. There was no time to explain all this. "He's really a very interesting character. It's just that he's always interesting in exactly the same way."

"So stay and help me!"

"I can't. My parents would be furious. They probably *are* furious."

Claire seemed to understand that. "All right. But couldn't you just turn the thieves into crickets and feed them to the blind owl, like you do in the book?"

"Claire, these men aren't the thieves from my story," said Sylvie.

"They're not?"

"They aren't even dressed the same. Different outfits altogether."

"I'm sorry. I only read the book once."

"Claire, these are *your* thieves. I'll try to help, but it's your dream." Sylvie gave the girl's hand a last squeeze, then jumped to the ground. "This time *you* get to do the Great Good Thing. Good-bye!"

And she hurried down the path the way she'd come.

Part Two

THE LAND TO THE EAST

chapter four

From then on, *The Great Good Thing* was the busiest book on the shelf. Claire would take it down at bedtime and read herself to sleep, sometimes leaving it open beside her. When that happened, Sylvie would look over to the east, beyond her father's forest, to see what sort of dream the Reader had come up with this time. No one else seemed to notice these distant vistas. It was as if they couldn't imagine any stories beyond their own and so couldn't see them when they appeared.

Sylvie *lived* for them. She'd never realized how confined she felt in her own story until she was finally able to break out of it. At first she felt guilty. What was wrong with her? Most characters would do anything to be a heroine.

Seeing how angry her parents were after The Adventure of the Muddy Forest, Sylvie learned not to mention her sightings of Claire's dream-world. If they didn't notice it, why bring it up? Instead, Sylvie would wander toward the eastern edge of the kingdom when no one was watching. This made her feel doubly guilty, because she loved her parents and had never been disobedient. Strong-willed, yes, but not disobedient. Still, the constantly shifting landscape beyond the eastern forest called to her so strongly, she just had to explore it.

Once, a whole city rose over the treetops, with towering glass buildings such as Sylvie had never imagined. When she arrived there she quickly became lost, but luckily the streets were empty and she could hear Claire's echoey voice calling her from blocks away.

Another time, the setting was a great metal-covered ship, propelled by some sort of machinery, without any sails or oarsmen at all. It was the same vessel, she learned, that Claire's mother and father had sailed away on, leaving the children for months in the care of their grandmother.

This afternoon, Sylvie looked past the sunny hills to what appeared to be an old house filled with moonlight. She waited until her father had withdrawn for his lute lesson, then headed down the usual wooded path to the edge of the kingdom.

She felt vaguely uneasy and glanced behind her as she went. Was it just her feelings of guilt? After a while, the dirt path dwindled to nothing in the underbrush, and she had to find her way by looking for the broken twigs and occasional footprints that she had left on earlier trips. She didn't notice a quiet figure following at a distance, stopping when she stopped, stepping behind trees whenever she turned to look back.

As always, her father's kingdom ended

abruptly, with just a narrow white space, like the margin of a page, before the new country began. Sylvie hesitated. The dark house before her, riding under the moon, looked somehow familiar, like a scene from her early childhood. But of course Sylvie had never had an early childhood.

Strange, she thought, and stepped across to a silvery lawn that sloped up to the porch.

The watcher remained hidden until Princess Sylvie had entered the house and let the door close behind her. Then, slowly, he stood.

Sylvie hurried through the dim rooms, whispering, "Claire, Claire."

"Over here."

She found her in an alcove beneath a curving staircase.

"My grandma's house," Claire explained. "She needs me."

A frail light led them to the second floor, their hands sliding along a gleaming banister. Across the landing they saw a half-open door, revealing lamplight within. Claire pushed the door open.

The canopied bed was empty, but had been slept in. A small lamp spread a yellow circle on the desk by the bay window. Claire immediately saw the pencilled note, a small, lined page torn from a notebook. No date or signature, just two words: FIND ME.

Claire murmured the words to herself, testing them on her tongue, then turned to Sylvie with frightened eyes. "What does it mean?"

"Did your grandmother write this?"

"I'm sure! Oh, Sylvie, I know she's been kidnapped!"

Sylvie pursed her lips. Somehow that didn't seem the way the story would go. Anyway, hadn't that part happened already, in The Adventure of the Muddy Forest? "Do you think," she said, "it could be a game? You know. Come and find me?"

Claire cocked her head to see if she was serious.

"Maybe not," said Sylvie. She picked up a small

framed photograph. Her breath caught in her throat. "Who's this girl?" she said. "I *know* her."

"You couldn't."

"It's the girl with the dark blue eyes."

"Sylvie, that picture was taken ages and ages ago. You're only—"

"I'm only twelve. But remember, I've been twelve since 1917. At least that's what it says at the front of the book."

Claire seemed to hold her breath. "You mean you knew my grandmother?"

"Well, I certainly know this girl. She read my story more times even than you. She was the first outside person I can remember looking at."

Claire stared at her. "You knew my grandmother!"

"I never said anything to her, but I wanted to. Sometimes I thought she knew more about me than I knew about myself. I always wondered about her."

"Well, she grew up."

"Grew up! Why? She was perfect as she was."

42

"I don't know, but she got real old. Here, look at this." Claire picked up another photo showing a gaunt woman standing behind a mild-looking couple with two children. "That's Grandma. That's my mom and dad. And that's Ricky and me."

Sylvie stared at the picture. "What a disguise!"

A tear glittered in the corner of Claire's eye. "How are we going to *find* her?"

"And how will we recognize her?" said Sylvie. "She might look like anything."

Claire reached an arm around Sylvie's shoulder. "Well," she said with a little smile, "we can go by the eyes."

"She didn't change them?"

"Still dark blue."

Sylvie looked again at the first photograph, the childish chin already firm with resolve, the gaze steady, with a hint of mischief. "I'm glad."

A distant booming sound made the girls look up. "The kidnappers!" cried Claire.

The booming grew louder, and Sylvie thought

she could hear the faraway voice of Claire's brother, Ricky. The edge of the room, up by the ceiling, was beginning to flake away. The house was falling apart!

"Got to go!" She squeezed Claire's hand, then ran out of the room and down to the ground floor as the stairs crumbled silently behind her. The walls and ceiling had grown thin as a cobweb, and she could see the moonlight through them. As she burst out the front door, she heard more booming sounds, and a voice, louder than before, calling, "Hey, sis, you better wake up! You're going to get it!"

The lawn became translucent green, then completely transparent as Sylvie ran down to the border and dove across into her father's woods. She grabbed at a solid tree root and clung to it till she caught her breath. Finally she lifted her head and looked back. The house and grounds had disappeared. There was nothing, not a window frame, a bird, or a star. Just absence, like an empty mind.

chapter five

The king was pacing outside the drawbridge when Sylvie arrived home, her dress dirty and her ribbons a disgrace. He marched her in and sat her down in a high-backed velvet chair right in the entry hall. The servants quietly withdrew.

Sylvie didn't know why her father was so angry. He was as angry as his character was ever allowed to get. Sylvie's mother, he said, his voice ringing through the vaulted room, had had an attack of the flutters and retired early. Did Sylvie realize how she was upsetting her parents? He forbade her to cross the eastern boundary again.

Sylvie looked at him curiously. "I did cross the boundary today," she said, "but how did you know?"

45

"Thank goodness someone cared enough to follow you. He said you almost didn't get back. Is that true?"

"Father, who is this caring person you're talking about?"

"That's hardly the point."

"You don't have to set spies on me. You know I'll tell you the truth."

"I didn't set spies on you. He took it on himself."

"Who?"

"Pingree."

"The jester? He has never cared about me since the day I was born."

"Well, thank heaven he cared about you today."

This was odd. Pingree had always made fun of Sylvie. He made fun of everyone, of course—it was his job—but there seemed an extra bite to his jokes about her, the princess with the muddy petticoats. His teasing could be merciless.

"Father, I'm sorry to have caused you all this worry. I didn't realize."

His look began to soften.

"But I can't promise I won't go again."

He stiffened up.

"I just can't. Everyone around here is so much older than I am. Pingree may not be any taller, but he's three times as old. And my story is always the same. Lovely, but the same."

"What's wrong with that?"

"I wish I could make you see how different everything is. I've never had such adventures before, or known someone actually younger than me, like Claire."

"What did you say?"

"That's her name. Claire."

"The Reader? You've been *talking* to her?"

"Oh, yes! She's very nice, but very sad. Her grandmother is sick. They took her to the hospital, but Claire seems to think somebody has kidnapped her. I keep telling her that stories all turn out fine in the end, but she doesn't believe me."

King Walther was silent a long time. "Have your tutors taught you nothing? Haven't you learned the first rule of the kingdom?"

"I know. *'Never look at the Reader.'* But nobody ever said why not."

"Go to your room!" he shouted. "You will not talk to this Reader again, do you understand?"

"Father!"

"I had no idea what danger you were putting yourself in. Putting us all in!"

"Oh, Claire isn't dangerous. She's younger than I am. She isn't dangerous at all."

"Not dangerous? She might step on you! How can you be friends with a giant?"

"Giant? Oh, no, she's my size. An ootch shorter, even."

"I've glanced up. I've seen her."

"You weren't supposed to." Sylvie smiled.

"Never mind!"

"But it's different, Father. Everything's different in a dream."

"How?"

"I don't know. Sizes even out."

"Whatever size she is, she's dangerous. Have

you ever thought," he continued, "what would happen if you got into trouble during one of those adventures of yours and couldn't get back?"

"I guess not." Then curiosity overcame her. "What *would* happen?"

"I hope we never find out."

Sylvie was silent.

"I think we almost found out today," he added darkly.

When Sylvie still would not promise, the king threatened to have her locked in her room. In the end he didn't do it, of course. His character wasn't conceived that way, and besides, how would she be able to run, on short notice, to any part of the story if she were locked in the castle? Storybook heroines must be able to move around at the flip of a page.

It was quite a while before the book was opened again. Everyone in the kingdom, even the goatherd, who had only a small speaking part, was glad for the rest. One of the older ladies-in-waiting expressed the hope that the Reader was growing tired of the story. The king and queen, for reasons of their own, agreed.

Sylvie felt on edge, almost afraid—feelings she never got to experience in her own story. She didn't talk to anyone about it, but she was sure something had happened. Thieves and kidnappers didn't concern her; they always got what they deserved. It was something about Claire herself, a sadness. No one in *The Great Good Thing* was sad for long. They were brave or cowardly, greedy or romantic, or generous or proud. Claire's sadness seemed a part of her.

"No more little jaunts in the woods?" the jester smirked as Sylvie passed him in the corridor outside the throne room.

"Why don't you jump in the Mere, Pingree?"

Each afternoon Sylvie made her way to the cliffs on page 35 and looked to the east. There were only her father's woods stretching to the horizon. On the evening of the sixth day, Sylvie was staring out over the Mere of Remind when she heard a familiar cry. A bright bird burst into the air, its wings catching the sunset. *"Reader!"* it rasped, and immediately the frogs in the Mere bassooned their alarm. Sylvie was on her feet running.

She hadn't far to go, since the Reader turned directly to Chapter Three, where Riggeloff's retainers and hired ruffians approach the castle at night and toss glittering Shawls of Slumber over the heads of the guards. But it was a strange thing. As the characters spoke their lines, another voice—Claire's, Sylvie realized—spoke the words with them, then went on to speak all the description in between. The thieves were unnerved at first, and glanced at one another. It had been years since anyone had read the book out loud. Luckily, Sylvie wasn't in this chapter. She ran to the parapet and hid in the shadows. Through the dark sky she could just make out the face of her friend, and behind her a glowing lamp.

After a few pages the Reader paused, and the thieves practically bumped into one another because of course they had to pause, too. As Sylvie watched, the sky narrowed to a sliver, and an enormous soft object, hairless and pink, slid onto the page, covering the drawbridge and pinning two thieves to the ground. A finger, Sylvie realized. Claire was holding her place! Sylvie heard the girl's muffled voice overhead: "Grandma? Are you awake?" Then the finger withdrew, and the book closed.

"What was *that* about?" the jester said, poking a nervous head out the window.

The king stepped onto the parapet. "You say you're friends with this creature?"

"She's really very nice."

"Tell her," snipped Pingree, "to use a bookmark next time. A plain, simple bookmark."

Sylvie went inside without a word.

The next afternoon, the book opened again,

this time to the chapter where Sylvie sets off on her quest to recover the treasure stolen by Riggeloff's men. Again she heard Claire's voice reading the words aloud as the characters relived their story. And again the girl chose the oddest place to stop. Riggeloff and his minions were galloping after Sylvie as she raced toward the cliff. The next instant they had to rein in their horses and stand around as if they had nothing to do.

"Grandma? Do you want me to keep reading?" came Claire's voice from the sky.

"Go on, dear," replied a voice so weak, Sylvie could hardly make out the words. "If you don't mind."

Claire picked up the book and began. She read almost to the end of the chapter, where Sylvie leaps from the cliff into the whirlpool. It's a dramatic scene, and no Reader ever stopped before the end of it, so Sylvie was surprised when the whirlpool suddenly lost its force and came to a standstill. She treaded water and looked up at

Prince Riggeloff on the cliff. He shrugged. Slowly she dog-paddled to shore.

"I think she's asleep," came the voice of Claire's mother. "It's so nice of you to do this."

"I *want* to." Claire was nearly whispering, but her words could be heard above the cliffs.

"Why don't you take a rest? Play a game with Ricky."

"He wouldn't." Sylvie could almost hear Claire's shrug. "I don't think he likes me, Mom."

"I'm sure that isn't true. Have you tried talking to him? Let him tell you about his treasure maps and his volcanoes."

"Those maps," said Claire, and her sigh made the tips of the pine trees sway.

"Come on, let's go and have some cocoa."

The sky darkened and went black. No one spoke until the backup lights came on. From all the opening and closing lately, the book's hinge was getting loose, and the lights weren't working properly. The sky came on green.

"Look at that," groaned the king. He called to the Chief Engineer and Mechanic, a big, bearded fellow in a greasy apron.

The man shook his head. "I'll do what I can, sire," he said.

"I rather like it," Sylvie said absently.

"A green sky?"

"Well, it makes for a change."

King Walther looked at her solemnly. "Are you getting tired of our little story?"

"Of course not!"

"Now that you've been having all these other adventures."

There was something in his eyes that made Sylvie go and hug him. "There's no story as good as this."

He patted her shoulder. "Thank you, dear, for saying so."

"Is that what you were worried about? That I'd find a story I liked better than ours?"

"Did you?"

She hesitated only a moment. "I'd never leave you and Mother."

"Without you"—he shook his head—"well, our story wouldn't make sense."

"Then we'll have to stay together."

"Even with the hinges?"

"I love those wiggly hinges. And the old blue-leather cover. And the tumbledown stone walls in the fields."

"We're getting those fixed."

"And the squeaky drawbridge."

"The drawbridge doesn't squeak."

"Father, it squeaks."

With that, all the lights went out, then sputtered on again. Yellow.

The next afternoon, Claire picked up where she'd left off and read aloud nearly to the end of the book. After an hour, her voice sounded raspy and she paused to rest.

"Do you think Grandma can hear you?" came her mother's voice.

"I don't know. I thought I saw a little smile a while ago."

"Claire." The voice paused. "You don't have to keep reading."

"I know."

"We could go for a walk. It's nice out."

"Maybe later."

Sylvie heard the woman's retreating footsteps. After a bit, Claire began to read again. "'The ancient Keeper of the Cave stepped out of the shadows, and Princess Sylvie saw him clearly for the first time, the thin, drawn lips, the fierce eyes, and most upsetting of all . . .'"

She broke off. The Keeper of the Cave looked around uncertainly.

"How's Grandma?" came a different voice.

Sylvie looked upward but could see nothing through the firelit roof of the cave.

"Asleep, I think."

"Then why are you reading?"

"In case she's not."

There was a long silence.

"It's her favorite book," Claire went on.

"If it's her favorite book, how come she gave it to you?" Another silence. "She's going to die, isn't she?"

"Shush, Ricky."

"She doesn't look so good."

Claire didn't reply. Then, in a soft voice, she did: "Why don't you read to her a little?"

"Me?"

"She would love it."

"I don't like that book," he said.

"Why?"

"It doesn't tell the truth."

"Just because it's not about volcanoes doesn't mean—"

"*You* read it. She wants you to read it. She gave it to you."

"That doesn't matter."

"She likes you."

"Ricky." Claire's tone was gentle. "She loves us both."

"No, she doesn't." His throat sounded tight. "No, she doesn't!"

"Who is it?" came the grandmother's thin voice.

"Nobody. It's just me."

"Ricky?"

"Hi, Grandma."

"Come closer. There you are."

"How ya doing?"

"Come give Grandma a hug." There was silence. "Why, you're trembling!" she said.

"Gotta go, Grandma." Footsteps barked on a bare floor, and a door slammed.

"He was *trembling*."

"He loves you very much, Grandma."

"Do you mind reading a little more, dear?"

Claire picked up the story in the Cave of Diamonds and continued to the end. All the characters were exhausted, but the book didn't close, so they all had to stay in their places. There was a great yawning sound, then nothing. Sylvie became concerned. She climbed the cliff and looked to the east. Beyond the edge of the kingdom lay a gray-white haze. By looking intently, she was able to make out a green shimmer. Leaves. A forest of white birch trees!

I *shouldn't* go, she thought, remembering how upset her father had been the last time. But something was wrong. Someone was in danger, she was sure of it.

I won't go far, she promised as she hurried down the path. Soon she was stepping across the white margin separating her father's brown forest from Claire's white one. Even the birds in this dream were white, with black-tipped wings. A white squirrel with a black nose scampered to the top of a silvery birch tree, then leaped to another birch, then another, the thin branches swaying wildly. Sylvie followed the squirrel and soon came to a clearing where four white tents stood in a semicircle. Claire emerged from one of them. She was dressed in a surgical gown, the cloth mask hanging loosely around her neck.

"My patient has disappeared," she said, too distressed even to say hello.

"I'll help you," said Sylvie. "But I can't stay."

Claire started through the forest, the ground covered with skeletal leaves. "We've got to find her!"

All the trees looked the same, the bark delicate and powdery as the skin of old women.

"Here's something." Sylvie picked up a dark blue stone, perfectly round, lying among the leaves.

"She left that for us!" cried Claire. "Come on."

"I really can't stay," said Sylvie. They pushed farther into the woods.

"Here!" Claire stooped and picked up a dark feather. It was the same unusual blue as the stone. "This must be the way."

The trees turned slowly as the girls passed.

"What's this?" said Sylvie. A swatch of silk, the same dark blue, hung from a thornbush.

"That's from her dress!"

There was a rustling sound ahead. Sylvie thought it was squirrels, but then she heard giggling, a girl's suppressed laughter.

Sylvie looked at her friend. "The girl with the dark blue eyes?"

Claire nodded. "She's here. She's right around here."

"We'll find her."

Thick laurel bushes, the leaves delicately curled and shining, blocked the way.

"Are you there?" Claire whispered, stepping closer. The bushes trembled. A breeze gusted up from the west, catching the underside of every leaf in the forest. Sylvie imagined she heard the distant sound of weeping.

Claire touched the thickly clustered leaves and gently pushed them aside. Laughing eyes, dark clear blue, looked out from the green darkness. "It's *you!*" Claire breathed.

Sylvie, too, felt a great happiness at the sight of

the girl. It was like seeing into her own heart. Of course she recognized her at once from the picture.

This was no picture. The girl was really here. But how *could* she be, as long as the grandmother was still alive? Unless . . .

"Play?" said the girl, her voice filled with excitement.

Now the sound of other voices, of voices crying and talking, grew louder in the wind. Sylvie looked around quickly. "I've got to go!" she realized with panic. She gave a last glance at the girl, then turned and ran.

The birches were disappearing all around her like white feathers plucked one after the other from the ground. She hadn't realized how far she had come. She would not have found her way at all if it weren't for the squirrel with the black nose who scampered ahead, leading her over ground that grew softer and softer underfoot.

There, just ahead, lay the dark, craggy forest

of her own country, but Sylvie found herself making less and less headway, although she was running harder than ever. She looked down. Her feet were sinking into the forest floor! Now she was ankle deep in—she didn't know what.

The ground was giving way all around her. As she reached the border, she suddenly felt herself sink to her hips, the lower half of her body invisible.

She cried out, reaching desperately to grab at a large stone projecting from the edge of her father's kingdom. For several seconds she clung to it, reassured by its roughness, so unlike the vagueness engulfing her.

"No," she moaned, feeling her fingers begin to slip. It was not fear she felt in those last moments, but anger and defeat. She who had never failed at anything was failing now.

"No!" she shouted, struggling furiously. Suddenly she lost her hold and plunged into nothing.

chapter six

Sylvie was no one, an absence within an absence, a blank in the center of her storied life. It's over, she vaguely thought, but no longer knew what was over. Images floated through her mind, devoid of meaning. A man with a crown, looking at her mournfully. A woman with a crown, weeping. Waves knocking against the shore. A burning tree, twisting with flame. Snow falling in water.

Were these nightmares? Memories? Past and future were equal, and equally meaningless. There was no up or down. She didn't even know she was falling until she heard a swift thumping sound, growing louder, then felt a sudden blow and a sharp pain in her shoulder, and realized that she had *stopped* falling.

"Ow! Ow!" she cried as the pain—it burned like a stab wound—brought her fully to her senses.

She was being lifted. The thudding was coming from just above her head. Reaching up, she felt powerful muscles sheathed in softness. Iron clamps gripped her shoulders.

The blind owl! She remembered now. It was the same huge bird she had once saved from the thornbush. Its talons had snagged the material of her cloak, but one claw had pierced her shoulder blade, which was afire with such pain that she could hardly breathe. As she was lifted higher, the princess saw the great rock she had clung to, then the thick woods of the kingdom.

She bit her lip as the bird carried her above the treetops, past the Mere of Remind, over the sheep pastures, outlaw encampments, and shepherds' huts toward the distant castle with the blue-and-white pennants snapping in the breeze.

The great bird sailed over the battlements and came down, beating its wings to slow its descent, on the narrow balcony outside Sylvie's chambers in the west turret.

"Ah, ah!" Sylvie shuddered as she felt a talon withdrawing, like a dagger being yanked from a sheath. After that she remembered nothing until she woke to the sound of knocking and realized she was in her own canopied bed, her shoulder aching and bandaged under her nightgown.

An old servant woman came in with a bowl of gruel and a cup of warm, foul-smelling liquid.

"What happened?" Sylvie said, still groggy.

The woman's narrow cheeks widened into a smile to see the princess awake. She told her how one of the chambermaids had found her unconscious on the balcony yesterday afternoon.

"Yesterday!"

What bothered Sylvie most was the fact that she had fainted. She was not a fainter. In the well-ordered world of her story, she was the one who rescued others who fainted.

"Perhaps you just fell asleep?" suggested the old woman.

"Yes, I was very tired."

And now she was hungry. She looked up from her second bowl of gruel to see her parents and the Keeper of Potions looking in through the door.

She had to tell them the truth, no matter how it upset them.

"But how," her father said after he had heard the story, "did the owl ever *find* you? It can't see."

"Well," said Sylvie, sitting up straighter in bed, "the owl is blind. That means it doesn't see boundaries. It didn't even know it was leaving the kingdom. It just heard me and came after me."

The queen leaned forward and lightly stroked her cheek. "Thank goodness it did," she said with a quaver in her voice.

"Don't you ever leave the kingdom again," said her father. "Promise me."

"I'm certainly not planning on it," Sylvie said with a tired smile.

After everyone had left, Sylvie remembered the little tremor in her mother's voice. She had never heard that before.

The princess was up and around by the next day, but the book remained closed. She didn't understand. Then she remembered the sounds she'd heard in the wind, the weeping and quiet talking. Suddenly she hated being trapped inside a closed book when Claire needed help. Claire was the sort of person who needed help often. She was not a heroine like Sylvie, but she was good-hearted. Sylvie liked feeling like an older sister.

In the mornings, the princess wandered among the peasants' cottages, where she petted the goats and lambs. Mostly she kept to herself. She wasn't a sad character and didn't know why she was sighing. Maybe she had caught something from Claire.

Her father was concerned about how quiet Sylvie had become and called for the Jester to cheer her up.

"Bad day!" rasped the little fellow, jumping up on the chair and smiling his smirky smile. "The vole ate her young, and then it stole your tongue!"

No response.

He strummed a sour chord on his dwarf-sized lute. "Your lute string come unstrung?" he sang shrilly, jumping onto the table and knocking over the health potion Sylvie was supposed to drink. "Your springs all come unsprung?"

Sylvie watched him do a little jig on the tabletop.

"Songs all gone unsung?" He arched his left brow.

No response. The truth was, she didn't care for

clowns, particularly this one. She couldn't understand how Readers ever found him amusing, yet they seemed to enjoy his antics, younger Readers especially. Maybe they were too far away to see him clearly. Something about his eyes—one was bright and lively, the other strangely dull. She never knew which to look at, or which reflected his real feelings. How different his jokes and puns were from the secret laughter in the laurel. Would she ever hear that sound again?

"Well," she said at last, getting up from her seat, "thanks at least for knocking over that awful potion." And she walked out of the room.

She didn't know how many days had passed since she'd seen Claire. There was an old clock in the tower and a sundial in the courtyard, but not a calendar in the kingdom. As a result, one might know to the minute what time it was without having the slightest idea about the month or year. Finally a bright-feathered bird lifted off from a turret and called its warning, and the frogs grumped in the bog. The book opened and Claire's face, looking a bit puffy, appeared overhead. She did not read aloud.

Sylvie heard her yawn several times and guessed that the girl was having her reading time before bed. Claire turned, as she so often did, to the chapter in which Riggeloff's thieves chase Sylvie to the cliff. Rather than let herself be captured, Sylvie flings herself into the Mere of Remind and is sucked under by the whirlpool. That's when the invisible fish comes to her rescue. And that is where, on this particular evening, Claire drifted to sleep, her hand still resting on the edge of the page.

Sylvie swam to shore and dried herself quickly with the monogrammed towel that hung just out of sight behind a bush. Then she changed into the fresh clothes that were always waiting for her. She wasn't going to disobey her parents, but maybe, if she climbed the cliff, she could get a glimpse of Claire's new dream.

At first there was nothing, then a whiteness within the nothing. The whiteness was moving, descending, like a great veil. Through it Sylvie could make out a backdrop of grays and greens. Water, she realized, a slowly breathing ocean, with snow falling into it.

She felt the pull of adventure, but forced herself to stay where she was. She remembered the quaver in her mother's voice.

Just then, she felt the ground shake slightly beneath her. The book was being lifted. Then darkness.

"Father!" Sylvie called out. She could see nothing at all.

A voice answered from the other cliff. "He's not in this section."

"Is that you, Prince?"

"No, this is Thomas."

Thomas was the one she thought of as "the nice thief," which was not a compliment. "Hello, Thomas. Could you run and find my father? I think something's wrong."

"I'll try. Can't see my blasted hand in front of my face."

Sylvie felt the ground bumping gently up and down beneath her. *Someone is carrying us!* she thought.

Then the motions stopped. Sylvie listened. Her father would arrive soon, and the backup lights would come on, and everything would be all right.

Without warning the book opened, and Sylvie found herself sliding to the right-hand side of the page. There was a sputtering sound, then a flaring light appeared, like the comet in Chapter Nineteen, only it was hot and grew hotter. A stench of smoke curled through the air. Behind the flame, Sylvie could make out the small eyes and round cheeks of Claire's brother, Ricky.

"Fire!" a voice called out, and soon other voices were shouting. Horses galloped through the shadowy underbrush.

"Princess!" Riggeloff cried, riding up to Sylvie

on his black horse, Thunder. "Don't go back to the castle. It's on fire!"

"Have you seen my parents?"

"I saw them running across the drawbridge!"

"Get them! Bring them here!"

"I will!" He turned the rearing horse and was gone.

Sylvie heard a voice from out of the swirling orange sky crying, "No, oh no!" It was Ricky's voice. "Ouch!" he yelled.

From what Sylvie could tell, the blaze had started in the west, near the front of the book. What would become of the ladies-in-waiting? They were never very good at taking care of themselves.

Soon the orange sky began to darken, and though the smoke still made her eyes sting, Sylvie realized the fire was dying down. A general cheer went up.

"It's gone out!" cried a woman's voice, quite nearby.

75

"Mother!" Sylvie called out. "Is Father with you?"

"Here!" King Walther called from the next page. He came through the underbrush, carrying a lantern, his crown pushed back on his head.

"Thank heaven we're safe!" the queen declared, holding her lapdog in the folds of her cloak.

But the smoking edge of the pages, not quite out, flared up again.

"Oh, no!" The queen's voice was shaking.

The sky bloomed yellow, and heat struck their faces.

"Quick!" Sylvie cried, pulling her parents to the edge of the illustration on page 35. "Get in the fish! He'll take us to the bottom of the Mere."

"Sylvie." Her father was shaking his head. "You don't understand . . ."

But then she did. The fire was only a few pages behind them, and Sylvie could see the Mere beginning to turn brown. It didn't look a bit wet. In another few seconds it would burst into flame.

"Over here!" It was Riggeloff's voice. "Climb up on Thunder!"

"Yes!" shouted King Walther. "Hurry!"

As Prince Riggeloff pulled Sylvie's parents onto the horse, Sylvie impulsively reached into the illustration and grabbed the gills of the invisible fish. Once out of the water, the creature was quite flat. She rolled it up like a great window shade, thrust it under her arm, and clambered onto the horse's back. Riggeloff set off at a gallop, heading south, away from the approaching flames.

Sylvie shouted, "No! Go east! Go east, Riggeloff!"

"What are you talking about?" he fairly snarled at her.

"The fire will get to us in the south! You can see that. Our only hope is the east."

"Nothing's there but the forest, and that's starting to burn!"

"Go through the fire if you must. The ocean is beyond it."

"Ocean?"

77

"Do it!" commanded King Walther.

Riggeloff cursed under his breath, but he yanked the reins and turned the whinnying stallion to the east, then set off, riding hard. Sylvie felt her teeth rattling in her head.

Several of the thieves, including Thomas, saw them go and leaped on their horses to follow. Pingree jumped on behind Thomas and grabbed hold of his coattails. The goatherd and one of the younger ladies-in-waiting ran after them.

A dull glow, like a bruise, could be seen through the trees up ahead. The air was fierce.

Riggeloff looked back at Princess Sylvie. "Keep going!" she shouted.

The farther they rode, the hotter the air became. "The path is going to catch fire!" he yelled.

"Go around it!"

Riggeloff looked at the king. He nodded grimly. Thunder's mane flashed as the great animal jumped from the pathway and crashed madly through the undergrowth.

"Oh!" Queen Emmeline cried as a branch lashed her cheek.

"Keep your head down!" said the king. "Faster, Riggeloff!"

"Watch out on the right!" Sylvie yelled, pointing to a curling flame just beginning to catch hold.

"Two fires now!" cried the prince, as the horse whinnied in terror.

"Go between them!" Sylvie yelled.

"Can't!"

"Do it!" commanded King Walther. Riggeloff dug his spurs into Thunder, and they flew through the forest. In the space between the two fires they could see a greenish haze.

"There it is!" cried Sylvie. "Straight ahead!"

The distant gray-green seemed more solid now, swaying before them. Even Riggeloff could see it was the ocean, and he gave a shout.

Up ahead, a burning pine tree groaned and twisted in the fire-whipped wind. It leaned, then leaned further and, with a great crack, fell in front of them, barring the way. The queen screamed as the stallion reared up, its eyes mirroring the flames.

"Can't get around!" Riggeloff shouted.

The king put his hand on the prince's shoulder. "Go over it!"

"What, sire?"

"Jump it!"

Riggeloff slowed the horse and took him in a wide circle, calming him with his voice. Thunder's flanks were trembling, his neck silvery with sweat. The prince stopped him for a few seconds. "Steady," he murmured. "All right!" He jabbed his spurs in, and the horse lunged ahead, straight into the flames.

A moment later they landed with a jolt on the other side and kept straight on at a gallop. Soon they arrived at the edge of the kingdom. Before them lay a great sea, and into it snow was falling.

No one spoke for some seconds. "Where . . ."

the queen faltered as her husband helped her dismount, "where *are* we?"

Sylvie came up and quietly took her hand. "We've come to the future."

Queen Emmeline looked back at her burning kingdom. A little mewing cry escaped her. Her right eyelash was singed, and her brown-and-white lapdog poked its nose from the folds of her cloak.

"Don't be afraid, Mother."

"What a choice," muttered Riggeloff. "Burn or drown."

"Wait," said Sylvie. "Maybe this will help." She began unrolling the invisible fish, no longer invisible but crinkly as a shed snake's skin.

"It looks dead," said the king.

"Let's see." Sylvie waded to her knees in the frigid water and laid the fish on the surface. It bobbed up and down like floating garbage. The king sighed. Then the fish began to absorb water and expand, growing wider and longer. They all

81

watched as it sank, with only its dorsal fin still floating on the surface. After a moment the fin slowly rose up, trembling, thickening.

The queen grasped her husband's arm.

"Yes, dear," he said. "It's coming to life!"

The fish swam in a slow circle and stopped beside Sylvie, its gills waving.

"It can't hold us all," said the prince. He turned and nodded as three thieves on horseback crashed toward them through the underbrush. Squirrels and other animals huddled at the water's edge. The tortoise was there, too. It stood like a great boulder lapped by sea waves.

"Three at most," said Riggeloff. "You, sire, and the queen, and of course the princess."

"What will you do?" said King Walther.

"Die. But first we will ride our horses out as far as they can swim."

The king looked solemnly at Riggeloff. "I have misjudged you."

"No, you haven't."

"You are a good man."

"I am a traitor. But our story has ended."

"I hope not."

"Get in, sire."

A hot wind blew at them from land, and they had no time to hesitate. "With your permission, dear fish," the king said, and the invisible fish opened wide its mouth. King Walther held his wife's hand and helped her in. "Now you, Sylvie."

Sylvie looked around with wild distress, seeing the goatherd and a lady-in-waiting staggering onto the beach, a wisp of smoke curling from her bustle.

"Let her get in!" Sylvie commanded Riggeloff. "I'll find another way."

"No, Princess. There's no story without you."

Tears sprang to her eyes. She knew he was right. "The tortoise!" she cried, jabbing her finger toward the shore. "He is the most powerful swimmer. Have everyone hold on to the edge of his shell!"

"I'll do it!" said Riggeloff. "Now get in!"

83

Sylvie took a last look at the kingdom she had lived in all her life. Fire was everywhere. She glimpsed a shadow overhead. It was the blind owl winging silently over the water.

"Good-bye," Sylvie whispered. She tasted salt in her mouth and realized that she was swallowing her tears. Her father touched her elbow. She nodded, then stepped into the fish's mouth. The king followed. The great jaws closed, the teeth fitting together perfectly to form a watertight wall, like glass. The creature sank beneath the surface and headed to sea.

Part Three

INTO THE MOUNTAINS

chapter seven

Far below the waves, the little family huddled together. They had no room to stand and hardly any to turn around. Every surface was slippery and smelled, not surprisingly, like fish. Queen Emmeline's lapdog whimpered, but for a long time no one spoke. Except for the steady swishing of the fish's powerful tail and the gurgling of its gills, the undersea world was silent. The royal passengers looked out the creature's transparent sides and thought their own thoughts. Had the others been able to escape? Sylvie wondered. What would become of them all when Claire woke up? It struck her forcefully: There was no book to go *back* to.

Finally, King Walther cleared his throat. "We

need to have a family council," he said quietly. "We don't know what may happen to us, but I want to say, while we have the chance—"

At first he couldn't say it, but he mastered his feelings and went on. "I want to tell you both, each of you, how much—" Again, emotion stopped him.

Queen Emmeline reached for his hand. "We've had a good life, Walther," she said. "And a truly wonderful story."

"I suppose all stories must end," he replied simply.

Sylvie couldn't stand hearing her parents talk this way. "Maybe the others survived. Some of them, anyway. We could start over."

The queen gave a little cry and flung her arms around her daughter's shoulders.

There, in the belly of the fish, with the gray confusion of water swirling around them, the family hugged one another, and for the second time that day Sylvie tasted tears in her mouth.

After what seemed an unbearable time, the

water outside began to grow brighter, and Sylvie realized the fish had risen near the surface. Sunlight zigzagged through the water, and a starfish drifted by. The queen's lapdog saw it and started barking—which is not the best thing to do when you're inside a fish, even an invisible one. The huge sea creature quivered violently from end to end, and the queen fell over. This, of course, excited the dog even more.

"Hush!" Sylvie hissed, scooping the wriggling animal into her arms.

"Hang on!" cried the king.

The inside of the quivering fish was as slick as the outside, but they managed to keep their balance, and soon the dog was quieted. The fish grew calm as well, then coasted on, its dorsal fin breaking the surface. At last it came to a gentle stop and bobbed about in the shallows.

The king looked at his family. "Dear ones," he said, "when we step outside we will be starting a new life. It may be short or long."

Queen Emmeline nodded, but Sylvie could see she was frightened.

"Let me go first," Sylvie piped up. "I've been in Claire's dreams before."

"No," said her father. "Whatever happens, I'd rather it happened to all of us at the same time."

"It's a little like being born," Sylvie said hopefully.

"Or dying," said the queen.

King Walther tapped gently on the roof of the fish's stomach. "We'll find out soon enough," he said. With a painful-sounding creak, the great jaws began to open. Warm sunlight streamed in, which felt good after their chilly journey, but they weren't used to the brightness.

Shielding their eyes, they couldn't immediately see the land they were stepping out on, or the person waiting there to greet them.

"Hello, everybody!" a voice called out. The happiness in the voice struck Sylvie as wonderfully familiar, and she wheeled around, squinting at a blue creature standing on the pebbly shore. "Sylvie, I knew you'd make it!"

"It's *you!*" Now that her eyes were getting used to the light, Sylvie saw that she hadn't been mistaken. The girl standing before her in a puffy-sleeved blue dress was the same young person she'd seen in the photograph in the moonlit house, and later, hiding among laurel bushes in Claire's dream.

"But I thought—" Sylvie began.

"What did you think, Princess Sylvie?" The girl with the dark blue eyes was smiling broadly.

"Well, didn't you die or something?"

"That's one way to look at it. Aren't you going to introduce me?"

"Oh! I'm sorry." She turned to her parents. "Mother, Father, I'd like you to meet, uh, Claire's *grandmother?*"

"That's way too complicated," said the girl. "Let's just say—well, how do *you* think of me, Sylvie?"

91

"I guess I always thought of you as our first Reader."

The girl laughed. "Very good! I like that."

"Were you really our first Reader?" asked King Walther.

"I'm sure of it."

The king and queen looked at each other. "Well!" said Queen Emmeline. "This is certainly a pleasure."

"Come on, let me show you around."

Sylvie had already been glancing behind the girl at what seemed a busy market town, with workmen hammering, kids running, and people generally hurrying about.

"Where exactly are we?" asked the king.

"In Claire's mind, of course. This is what you'd call the backstage area," she said, leading the bewildered family through the streets. "Up ahead there, where you see the bright spotlights, that's where Claire has her dreams."

"Really?" said Sylvie. As they drew closer,

the lights in the dream area began dimming down to a midnight blue. In the center of the space stood a many-gabled Victorian house that appeared to be bathed in moonlight.

"I've been there!" Sylvie exclaimed.

"Impossible," said Queen Emmeline. "We just came across an ocean!"

"I think you'll find, Your Highness," said the girl with the dark blue eyes, "that distance isn't very important here. I see you're just in time. Claire needs you in this one."

"This what?" said the queen.

"This dream. Follow me."

"But I don't know my lines!"

"Oh, you don't need to worry about that."

"I never go on without knowing my lines."

"You may not have any. This is going to be one of those short, just-before-waking dreams."

"But, my hair!"

"Dear," said the king, laying a reassuring hand on his wife's shoulder, "we may as well learn

93

about this now as later." He turned to the girl. "Tell us what to do."

"Just go up there and—react."

"React?" said the queen. "I don't react."

"Then act."

"Come, Mother," said Princess Sylvie, "it'll be fun."

"Here," said the girl with dark blue eyes, "I'll take the dog." She remained outside the circle holding the lapdog while Sylvie and her parents stepped onstage. At first they were the only ones there; then Claire appeared at the top of the curving staircase. She was wearing a black dress and carried a single marigold. It was odd to see her all dressed up, as if she'd just returned from a grown-up party where she hadn't had much fun.

"You came!" Claire cried, hurrying down the stairs. "And you brought your parents."

"Mother, Father," said Sylvie, "I'd like you to meet Claire."

Claire curtsied, and Sylvie's parents gave a

regal nod. "How did you find your way here?" she asked the queen.

Queen Emmeline's face froze with fear. Clearly, she was supposed to say something.

"Did you come on foot? By carriage?"

The queen's voice remained frozen in her throat.

"By fish," Sylvie put in.

A distant ringing sound reached them from upstairs, and suddenly Claire disappeared. The lights began dimming.

The girl with the dark blue eyes signaled to Sylvie. "That was Claire's alarm clock. You'll need to get prepared."

"Prepared for what?" the king asked in a stage whisper.

"For Claire's waking up."

"Will we die?" said Queen Emmeline, finding her voice at last.

"Oh, I don't think so. Of course, there's never been a situation like this before."

"You're saying you don't know?"

"Afraid not."

"So we *could* die."

"It isn't so bad. I've done it myself. Why don't you all hold hands? It's easier to keep track."

"Keep track?" said the king.

"As you disappear."

The king, queen, and princess held each other's hands tightly. "I love you!" Sylvie whispered as she watched her parents fading away. Then she began to disappear, too. She felt the pressure of their hands but could see nothing. In that moment she had a brief vision: a night table with a picture frame, and a window behind it with the shade pulled down. Then that, too, faded, and everyone turned visible again, off-duty until the next dream.

"Thank God!" said the queen, when she saw they were all right.

As they stepped from the performance area, Sylvie noticed that the spotlights had been turned out. In fact, the house had disappeared, and a man was sweeping the stage with a push broom.

"This is going to take some getting used to," said Sylvie.

A commotion made them turn around. To their amazement, Prince Riggeloff rode up on Thunder.

"You're here!" cried the king.

"The better to plague you, sire," said the prince with a slight smile. "I saw you up on the stage," he said. "You've certainly made yourselves right at home."

"Did the others get here?" Sylvie asked.

"Some. You should have seen Pingree. While the rest of us were hanging on to the edge of the tortoise, that little monkey was sitting on top of the shell giving orders to everybody."

A dozen characters, he said, including several thieves and shepherds and one lady-in-waiting, had clung to the edge of the wide shell and been towed across the water.

It had been quite a day for all of them. But the good news, Sylvie realized, was that being left in the mind after the dreamer wakes up was not so different from being left inside a book after the Reader has closed it and put it back on the shelf. It wasn't *really* the same, of course, especially during that odd in-between time when the buildings and people turned transparent and one could see both waking and dreaming worlds at once.

She didn't have much time to ponder this. From the time of their arrival, the survivors of the Great Crossing were often in the Reader's thoughts, and usually in her dreams, along with characters who had never set foot in *The Great Good Thing*. School friends of Claire's made occasional appearances, and in one episode Claire's mother and father could be seen wandering distractedly by a lake tossing bread to the goldfish. In another dream, Ricky appeared in the shape of a puffy lizard with green eyes. Everyone cheered when he skittered into the mouth of a red-bellied water snake. The fact that he reappeared in the dream after next didn't lessen the feeling of satisfaction in the least.

There were other things to get used to, particularly the abrupt way that scenes changed and people got around. In one dream, Claire and Sylvie were climbing a long stairway when they noticed the steps behind them had caught fire. They ran faster, but the fire was catching up. The stairs ended in midair, and the friends jumped off—and flew! For a while, most of their adventures involved fire, like the time Sylvie pulled a handkerchief out of her pocket and it burst into flames.

Then there were the crowds. Dozens of characters milled around between dreams. It was like being backstage at a grand opera. Never had Sylvie seen this many people, pets, buildings, and ball gowns. When she tripped over a scurrying weasel that had been run over by a wagon and killed several dreams ago, she went to look for her friend with the dark blue eyes. Thank goodness she was there to explain how things worked.

"Once dreamed," said the girl, "a character never completely disappears, because everything the mind creates is permanent." She smiled at Sylvie's look of surprise. "Naturally, if certain characters aren't called on for a long time, they tend to wander off and explore other parts of the country. I bet that funny little weasel will disappear in the bushes one of these days, and we may never see him again."

"Other parts of *what* country?"

"You didn't think this town was all there was? The mind's a big place. This is just the part Claire's aware of. What about everything she's forgotten? Or the things she's afraid to think about? There's a whole country out there."

"Sounds exciting."

"I thought you'd say that."

Sylvie's parents were having entirely too much excitement right here in town, and they didn't care for it. It is not easy for older people to give up the words they've lived by. What upset Queen Emmeline most was making up her own dialogue. Sylvie tried to convince her that all she had to do was look straight into the eyes of the character facing her and speak her mind. The queen had never had trouble doing that in the old book when the covers were closed and nobody was around except the family. She just couldn't do it when everyone was watching.

Often the queen and her subjects reverted to the dialogue they knew best, and everyone enjoyed it when that happened, although there weren't enough characters to put on a full-scale production. Riggeloff had only a handful of thieves to command, and the queen found she had just a single lady-in-waiting, the young one who'd been strolling in the woods with the goatherd when the fire broke out. Of course, the owl and the invisible fish were here, and the giant tortoise that had saved so many of them on the day of the fire. But one never knew when a stranger might pop up and throw the dialogue off. The character named Ricky was especially troublesome. Even Prince Riggeloff avoided him after a disastrous episode when he tried to get the boy to join the band of thieves. Ricky demanded to *lead* them.

No one minded, though, when Claire appeared. She was very nice, and these were her dreams, after all. Often her young friend with the dark blue eyes accompanied her. The first time King Walther saw them together sauntering through the marketplace, his face brightened and he called out cheerily. The king was always gracious, but no one who had known him in the old book would have called him cheery. Sylvie got the feeling he liked having young people around. She did, too, of course. In fact, the three girls sometimes fell into fits of silliness that left them limp from giggling.

They were different, though. Sylvie realized this one day when she asked Claire if anyone lived beyond the eastern gate of the town. Claire had no idea, and it was obvious she didn't want to know. She was afraid to know. She was afraid of

102

so many things. Gradually, although she would never say it, Sylvie came to feel the limitations of her friend. When she thought of the girl with the dark blue eyes, she could sense no limits at all.

Time went on, and no one kept track of it. Eventually, a number of strangers began appearing in the dreams—boys who were no longer children, then young men who were no longer boys—and the games and adventures tapered off. The day came when Sylvie and her family found themselves watching from a distance while Claire failed algebra tests, or found just the right words to shout at her brother, or walked in the herb garden with pimply young men.

Strange objects crowded the stories, and plots that made no sense. One morning King Walther looked out his window and found the entire eastern meadow covered with envelopes. The groundskeeper brought in a big hamper of them. PAST DUE, they were marked. PAST DUE, PAST DUE.

103

Another time, Claire, now a young woman, stepped onto a stage to give a speech before a crowd of strangers. No one had thought to invite Sylvie and her friends, and they had to stand in the back. Even from there they could see the panic on Claire's face. She had forgotten the words of her speech. In fact, she'd forgotten to get dressed—all she had on was her underwear! The king quickly handed his robe to Sylvie, who struggled through the crowd to bring it up to her friend. But there were too many elbows and shoulders, and before Sylvie reached the stage, Claire had fled in tears.

"Some story!" muttered the king.

It was shortly after that incident that the girl with the dark blue eyes placed a small white box in Sylvie's hands. It held a gold locket on a thin chain.

"Thank you!" Sylvie rubbed her thumb over the fancy S engraved on the front, then clicked the locket open. "It's a picture of you!"

"To remember me by," the girl said with a small smile.

"Remember you? I see you every day!"

"Still."

Sylvie felt puzzled by the conversation, but what really disturbed her were Claire's chaotic dreams. After a particularly upsetting one, she spoke privately to her father. "You know what we need to do, don't you?"

"What do you mean?"

"I hear this is a big country."

"Oh?"

"Mostly unexplored." She looked at him meaningfully.

He began fiddling with his mustache. "I know things haven't been going as well as they might lately. . . ."

"Father."

"All right, things have been dreadful. But you'll never get your mother to agree to go. She likes what she knows."

"I like what I don't know."

"I have noticed."

"But none of that's important. We've got to look ahead."

"I don't know how to look ahead."

"I do," said Sylvie. "There's no future for us here. Claire is growing up. Like it or not, she is forgetting us."

The king was silent. "Let me think about this," he said at last.

The next day King Walther called together all the characters who had come over from *The Great Good Thing*.

"We all love Claire," he declared, and there was a general murmur of agreement. "And we are grateful to her for welcoming us in our time of trouble. But the time has come now to get on with our lives."

The queen tightened her grip on Sylvie's hand. Riggeloff nodded.

"Princess Sylvie's friend has been telling her

about the rest of this country. While we've been staying in this one town, there's a whole wilderness beyond the eastern gate." The king looked out over the crowd. "What do you say we go out and explore it?"

"Hear, hear!" cried several soldiers. That was the only dialogue they ever had, so no one took them seriously until Riggeloff added his own deep voice to theirs.

"I have spoken with the queen, and she is in agreement," said King Walther.

Barely in agreement, thought Sylvie. She had listened outside their chamber last night. It had taken her father hours to convince her.

"Tomorrow morning, then," he continued, "we leave for the interior. I can't tell you what we will find, or the dangers we may face. It is my hope we'll find a place where we can rebuild our lives and relive our story in peace."

"Hear, hear!"

Sylvie couldn't sleep that night. At last! This

was what she was made for, to risk all, to do great deeds, not to live a safe life as a secondary character in somebody else's dreams! And now she wasn't even *in* those dreams.

And so the next morning, King Walther and all his subjects, loaded with provisions and mounted on fresh horses, started along the road leading into the countryside. They made quite a sight, almost like a circus leaving town, with their gay banners flying, dogs and children running alongside, and the townsfolk waving good-bye.

The great tortoise, his head and feet withdrawn, was pulled by two horses on a specially built cart. The invisible fish, rolled up and marked FRAGILE, bounced along atop a teetering pile of crates. Queen Emmeline, holding her little dog, kept glancing back at the receding buildings, but everyone else was looking ahead, anxious to see the new landscape. The jester, his bright eyes flashing in the morning sunlight, was in particularly high spirits and kept shouting out jokes that made the guardsmen laugh, although the king's smile was tight and his eyes alert.

Sylvie stuck her head out the coach window, loving the feeling of warm wind against her face. Overhead, she noticed, the blind owl was gliding on upper currents. It was a fine day to start a new life.

Waiting at the town's gate stood her friend with the dark blue eyes. She waved.

"Will we see you again?" Sylvie cried, leaning out the window.

"Of course," the girl said gaily.

"Will you take care of Claire?"

The girl nodded. "That's my job."

The two looked at each other as the dusty road stretched out between them. "Find me!" Sylvie called out suddenly, just before the road took a bend.

"I will!" called the girl.

"Find me! Don't forget!"

Long afterward, Sylvie would remember the white little hand in the distance, waving and waving.

chapter eight

Life was hard in the mountains. Sometimes it was close to terrifying, even for Sylvie, who was not easily scared. Sheltering in a cave while a windstorm swore at them outside, Sylvie longed to be back in the well-lit streets of Claire's dreams, or among beach umbrellas in the side-alleys of her daydreams. Queen Emmeline was miserable. Her dresses were getting wrinkled, and her hair was hopeless. How easy it had been living in a bustling town, with nothing to worry about but one's entrances and exits. Here, nothing was certain. A mountain path ended in a shaggy cliff. A stream turned out to be bedded in quicksand, and before the travelers could turn back, it swallowed a screaming horse and very nearly its rider.

Yet there were scenes of incredible beauty, including a whole skyful of sunsets that Claire had once dreamed about or seen somewhere and since forgotten, sunset behind sunset behind sunset. And tiny things like blue clover in summer rain.

How could Claire ever have forgotten that clover! thought Sylvie. But of course, she realized, one can't remember everything. Apparently, she didn't even remember Sylvie.

That thought began to gnaw at her. If Claire no longer remembered their story, who would? Was the day coming when no one in the world would remember *The Great Good Thing*? Maybe this expedition wasn't such a good idea. The farther they plunged into the wilderness, the less likely it was that anyone would *ever* find them.

Sylvie didn't confide her fears, and they didn't seem to occur to anyone else. It alarmed her, somehow, whenever some character from Claire's past dreams came by. These creatures, whether human or animal, would pass in silence, eyes to the ground. They didn't look well. Some had reddish scabs on their bodies, and several walked with a limp. Sylvie thought of them as the Disappointed Ones, beings who didn't have an existence outside of Claire's mind and didn't know what to do now that they were no longer thought about. Sylvie closed her eyes tight and promised herself *never* to become a Disappointed One.

She spoke to her father about taming some of the healthier creatures and taking them along. It would be a shame to leave them out here.

"You're welcome to try."

So Sylvie lured them with bits of food and soft words. When one got close enough, she reached out to touch the angry rash on his forehead. Then she drew back her hand with a little gasp. It was not a rash. It was not a rash at all. It was *rust*.

112

Many of these lost creatures, she found, were unsavable and had to be driven off. These were the ones with the most extensive red patches. There was no doubt about it; they were rusting away. A few had rusted all the way through.

But others, whose skin was still clear, seemed grateful to be thought useful. By the time the king's caravan approached the third southern mountain, the company was larger by several boys, a children's librarian, a geometry teacher, and two of Claire's long-forgotten aunts. Along with them, baaing and flapping, came three sheep and a cloud of swallowtail butterflies.

In all their time in the wilderness, Princess Sylvie never had a visit from Claire, but she could hardly expect visitors in such a remote place. They settled in a secluded valley, a land offering streams, protection from storms, and enough room to start rebuilding the castle as it once had been. There was even a modest lake that might serve as a new Mere of Remind. The young men recruited from the Disappointed Ones proved willing workers, hauling stones by ropes and pulleys up to the stonemasons working on the north face of the castle. The geometry teacher, a rail-thin fellow named Norbert Fangl, became Sylvie's tutor. The aunts and children's librarian found jobs as ladies-in-waiting. There had been a great need for ladies-in-waiting ever since the day of the fire.

It was a time of enterprise, and Sylvie was kept busy riding about the new country with her father and working out plans. Still, at night or on rainy afternoons when the work couldn't go forward, she'd sit by her window and open the golden locket her friend had given her. At times it unnerved her to look at it, because the picture kept changing. For every time she'd see the smiling girl, there would be times when a marmalade-colored cat would appear, or a gaunt old woman, or a blue dragonfly.

Occasionally, at royal command, a new production of *The Great Good Thing* would be staged. This was not just for entertainment. Everyone needed to be kept in practice and up to performance level. After all, there was no book to refer to anymore; the characters had to remember their own lines. They didn't always do a good job. Queen Emmeline, for one, was growing forgetful. After her experiences in Claire's dreams, where she'd had to make up her own dialogue, she got the story mixed up in her head.

Thomas kept breaking out of character to fetch things for Sylvie or pay her compliments. Once he brought her a rose.

"Steal!" shouted Sylvie. "Steal and pillage! Don't bring me roses!"

The character who strayed most often from the text was Pingree the Jester. He'd come up with different quips, new tricks and puns, whenever he came onstage. The king reprimanded him, but Pingree didn't stop. "There's nothing older than an old joke," he replied when challenged. "It's just not funny the tenth or twentieth time."

"It wasn't funny the first time," Sylvie murmured under her breath.

"What was that, dear?" said King Walther.

"Nothing."

"Nothing comes of nothing, Sylvie. This is a book. We have to say everything."

"My very point!" piped Pingree. His bright eye seemed to sparkle, while his dull eye blinked slowly. "This is *not* a book. This may not be a book ever again. Why do we have to follow the words of that moldy old story? We can make up better ones on our own."

King Walther grabbed the little man by his green felt collar and shook him till his cap fell off. "What did you say?" he growled.

"Well, I mean . . ."

"Without our story, our wonderful, magical, astonishing old story," continued the king, "we are nothing! And if *we* are nothing, what does

116

that make *you?*" He gave the jester a shove that tumbled him backward over an ottoman.

For a while afterward, Pingree behaved, speaking his lines as written. But it seemed to Sylvie that he had an especially secretive look these days. When she saw him slip off into the forest one afternoon, she followed, ducking out of sight whenever he looked back. To her amazement, he clambered up the rocky path to the thieves' encampment. Riggeloff's second in command, a bull of a man named Hroth, came out of the black silk tent and shook Pingree's hand. Sylvie couldn't hear what they were saying, but the conversation was entirely too cordial, she felt.

That afternoon something happened that made her forget all about Pingree. The stonemasons were hammering away when a sentry caught sight of a distant figure coming down into the valley. The alarm sounded, and everyone raced to the parapets. The visitor was on horseback—no, on a donkey—but it wasn't until the rider had crossed the wooden drawbridge that they saw it was a girl, her features hidden in her cloak. A crowd circled her as she rode into the courtyard, dismounted, and threw back her hood.

"You found us!" Sylvie cried, rushing to her friend with the dark blue eyes.

The girl laughed. "I told you."

"Welcome, dear friend," declared King Walther, grasping her hand.

A celebration banquet was arranged, with dancing, jesting, and of course storytelling. Afterward, the girl spoke to the royal family in private and told them that Princess Sylvie was needed back in the city at once.

"Not the rest of us?" said the queen.

The girl gave a small smile and a slight shake of her head.

"Well," said King Walther, "at least she has remembered one of us."

This was fine news, but also troubling. If Sylvie left the kingdom they were building, would she return? And if she were being called back for just one or two dream stories and then forgotten again, how would that make her feel? Better to stay where they were safe and could relive their own story anytime they wanted.

"After all," King Walther said, "didn't you tell us that once a character has been dreamed, he lives forever?"

"In a way," said the girl.

"Well, then," he said, "we could go on living here forever!"

But Sylvie, being who she was, felt impatient to return with her friend and see what adventures awaited her, and in the end, her parents, being the characters *they* were, could not say no.

Later that night, a messenger knocked lightly on Sylvie's door to say that her tutor, Professor Fangl, would like to speak with her.

A moment later, the angular geometry teacher slipped quietly as a bookmark into the room. "I hear that you're going back to town," he said.

"Tomorrow morning."

"I wonder, Your Highness," he said, "if you might put in a word for me with Miss Claire."

"What do you mean?'

He was holding his hat and fiddling with it nervously as he spoke. "If you'd just remind her of me?"

"You want to be in her dreams again!"

"Yes, Your Highness, if you don't mind."

"But I need you, Fangl. You were teaching me about parallelograms."

"A very important shape, I'm sure," he said, turning his hat around and around. "Especially here."

"Why here especially?"

"Well, here everything's parallel to everything else. I've made a study of it."

"Really! We'll have to talk about this."

"Yes, Your Majesty."

She looked at him a moment. "Aren't you happy here, Fangl?"

"Oh, very. It's just—" He seemed embarrassed.

"I'm not sure about my health lately."

"We have doctors."

"Not for this." He lifted a lock of his limp hair to reveal a small discoloration on the side of his forehead.

"What is it?"

"I think you know."

She stepped closer. It was a rough, reddish patch of skin. She gave a little gasp.

"Yes," he said. "We both know the signs."

"We've got to get you back in Claire's dreams right away!"

"Thank you, Your Highness. Frankly, I'm glad you're going back, as well."

"Why?" Sylvie glanced quickly in the looking glass. "Am I starting to rust, too?"

"Oh, I'm *sure* not. Anyway, you came to Claire from outside, from a book. There must be other copies."

"Do you think so?"

"It's customary."

121

"But what about you? Isn't there an actual Norbert Fangl?"

"Mr. Fangl died six years ago. I'm Claire's memory of him."

"I'm sorry."

"It's all right. As we know, memories have a life of their own."

"Are you saying I'm a memory, too?"

"Of course. You're Claire's memory of your story. That's what worries me."

"What do you mean?"

"The shape of the story has been changing. Have you noticed? A shame, really. I was fond of the old shape."

"Hold on. Just because a lady-in-waiting forgets her lines once in a while . . ."

"That wouldn't change the shape. Keep your eye on the shape."

"What are you saying?"

He bowed and moved toward the door. "Just keep your eye on the shape."

chapter nine

Next morning, the king and queen were on hand to say good-bye. Sylvie climbed up on the donkey behind the girl with the dark blue eyes, and the footman handed her up a big basket of provisions.

"Good-bye, everyone! I'll be back as soon as I can," Sylvie called. Then they started off. She was braced for a hard journey through the mountains. After all, it had taken her family many weeks to find their way to this valley. But somehow it took hardly any time for Sylvie and her friend to arrive back in town. No sooner had the banners of the castle disappeared behind them than the glint of steel-and-glass buildings flashed up ahead.

The place had changed amazingly in the time Sylvie had been away. It was no longer the small market town she had left, but a real city, with strange vehicles zooming about at unimaginable speeds. Sylvie's companion dismounted and held the rope while Sylvie hopped down. "Claire needs you," said the girl. "But it's not for a dream."

"What, then?"

"She needs you to tell a story." She smiled at Sylvie's confusion. "Come on."

Sylvie squinted up at the noon sun as they started off. They turned down a side street, leading the donkey by its rope. They turned left, then left again, and again left. At each turn the street grew narrower and the sky above them darker.

Sylvie looked up in wonder. "Why is the sky getting darker?"

"The lighting always changes when we go deeper."

"But we're not going down."

124

"Not deeper that way, deeper toward the center."

"The center?"

"Of Claire's story. You'll see."

Left again, and left, left, left, in smaller and smaller squares. Finally there was no further turn to make, and they found themselves before a dark Victorian house surrounded by a moonlit lawn.

"The house from the dream," said Sylvie.

"Yes."

They let the donkey graze out front, and mounted the steps. The front door was unlatched and the hallway dark. Above them, a weak light gleamed along the curving banister to the second floor. The girls started up.

"These stairs didn't squeak last time," whispered Sylvie.

"That was a long time ago."

"It was?"

"It was also a dream."

125

"You mean this isn't?"

"No," said the girl, laying her hand lightly on Sylvie's wrist. "We're going upstairs into Claire's real life."

Sylvie looked at her in astonishment. "Will I be all right?"

"Yes. With me with you."

"Will I be able to get back?"

The girl reached out and swept a strand of hair from Sylvie's forehead. "With me with you," she said again. "Come on."

They continued up the stairs. "Whose house is this?" Sylvie asked.

"Mine. But Claire lives here now."

They reached the landing. The door across the way stood partly open, throwing a wedge of light on the floor.

"I remember that room," said Sylvie.

"Listen."

Sylvie closed her eyes to catch the voices. Two voices. Sylvie's face brightened to realize that one of them was Claire's.

"Tomorrow we'll go," the voice was saying. "I promise." When there was no answer, Claire continued. "Don't you want to go?"

"We've already taken out all the good books."

"Well, all the storybooks. But there are all kinds of other books at the library. And you have that big book on tornadoes your uncle Richard gave you."

"I only like stories."

Sylvie and her friend slipped into the room. A large, comfortable-looking lady in a green bathrobe sat on the bed beside a little girl Sylvie had never seen before.

"So do I," said the lady in the bathrobe, squeezing the child's shoulder. "But what kind of people would we be if we never learned anything about tornadoes or elections?"

"Happy?"

"Happy! That's my goosie."

Sylvie stared at the woman. Claire's voice, she was sure of it, had come out of her mouth.

"Tell me a story, Mommy."

127

Sylvie turned to the girl with the dark blue eyes. "What a disguise!" she whispered.

"In a few years it will get even better," her friend whispered back.

The woman was telling her daughter that she didn't know any stories.

"You must know some," said the child. "You said you used to read a lot."

"I used to. There was a book I would read all the time, over and over. But something happened to it."

"What?"

"I can't remember."

"Tell it to me!"

"I can't remember, Lily! Don't push me!"

The girl was silent.

"What did she call her?" whispered Sylvie.

"Lily. She wanted to name her after you, but she couldn't remember your name."

"How can that be? We've been in her dreams."

"She doesn't remember her dreams. There

128

were too many fires in them, so she stopped remembering."

"Can she see us?" Sylvie whispered.

"Not out here."

"But I'm in plain sight."

"You don't exist."

"I certainly do!"

"Not out here."

Sylvie looked around in wonder. So *this* was the world Readers lived in when they weren't reading. "Really!" she whispered. "Can she hear me?"

"Only if she's very quiet."

Sylvie's attention was drawn to Claire's daughter, who had begun to sniffle.

"I'm sorry," said Claire. "I'd tell you the story if I could. Maybe we could read one of your old books."

"Never mind."

The girl with the dark blue eyes gave a tug at Sylvie's sleeve. Sylvie stepped to the head of the bed, beside the gauzy curtain. Claire was still

Claire, she realized, now that she saw her up close. She was still plain looking, but somehow less plain than she'd been as a child. Her body was soft and a little heavy, but friendly. She'd grown into her over-wide mouth, and there were little smile lines around it, suggesting that her life had not been unhappy.

"It's called," Sylvie began, then cleared her throat. "It's called…"

Claire lifted her head triumphantly. "It's called *The Great Good Thing*."

"What is, Mommy?"

"Oh!" said Claire. "I remember how it felt holding that little book. Soft blue leather! I remember how it smelled. Dust and rose petals. Mostly dust, really."

"Tell me the story! You've got to tell me!"

Claire shook her head.

Sylvie stood in the shadows at the head of the bed. Her voice was a murmur. "The princess stood before the king. 'Father,' she said…"

"'Father,' she said." Claire spoke in a firm voice. "'I cannot marry Prince Riggeloff.'"

"Wriggle?"

"Don't interrupt." She paused and looked down at her hands.

Her daughter watched her.

Sylvie murmured, "'Not marry Riggeloff?' cried the king . . ."

"Cried the king," said Claire. She closed her eyes tight. "'Not marry Riggeloff?' cried the king. 'For heaven's sake, child, he is handsome, rich . . .' 'Kind, brave,' continued Princess Sylvie, 'yes, I am aware of his qualities.'"

The girl waited.

"Aware of his qualities," Claire said, half to herself. "Isn't that wonderful?"

"Don't interrupt, Mommy!" They both laughed.

With Sylvie's prompting, Claire stumbled on, finally getting to the end of the story where the thieves are turned into crickets and the horrible Keeper of the Cave turns into a prince. It took hours, and her daughter fell asleep in Chapter Nine, but Claire kept going, with wonder in her voice and sometimes tears in her eyes. Afterward, she snuggled down, her lips curved in a smile. She looked pretty, Sylvie thought.

Outside in the hall, Sylvie's friend came up to her and kissed her on the cheek. "Tonight you have done another Great Good Thing," she said.

"I didn't really do anything."

"Perhaps not," said the girl, "but would you do it again tomorrow?"

"You think Claire still needs me?"

"Yes. She remembers the story now, but not every word of it."

"Why should she remember every word?"

"You'll see."

"You do like to be mysterious."

"I'll be even more mysterious. You need *her*. This is the first time your story's been told by someone out here since the time of the great fire."

"That's true," Sylvie said thoughtfully. "But

we've been putting on productions in the wilderness, to keep in practice."

"They're full of mistakes."

"You mean," Sylvie said, remembering the Geometry teacher, "the shape's been wrong?"

"I mean your story is falling apart."

Sylvie was taken aback to hear her usually cheerful friend speaking this way. "What can I do?"

"Remember every word. Every comma. And help Claire remember."

"All right."

"It's life or death."

"Why does it matter so much to her?"

"Not to her. It's life or death to *you!*"

Sylvie stared at her friend.

The girl patted her shoulder. "Just stay."

So Sylvie stayed. Nearly every night for the next few weeks she stood by the head of the bed behind the gauzy curtain and prompted Claire whenever she hesitated or put words in the wrong character's mouth. Claire's daughter, Lily, fell in love with the story, of course—who would not?—and demanded to hear it over and over. Before long, the girl was correcting her mother whenever she left out a phrase, or even a word. Once or twice, falling asleep at her mother's side, Lily actually dreamed about the story. Of course, since she'd never seen the original book, she had all the costumes wrong.

One evening, Sylvie found Claire and Lily sitting at the big desk doing arithmetic. The child was a whiz at subtraction, a concept Sylvie had always had trouble with. If something was there, how could it disappear? If something had happened, how could it not happen?

She watched them awhile, then bent and whispered the word, "Parallelogram."

Claire looked up, thinking of something.

"Mommy, you're not doing the problem!"

"Sorry, dear. Where were we?"

A tall man came in then and set cups of hot chocolate in front of them. "How's it coming?" he said, giving Claire's shoulder a squeeze.

"Daddy, we're borrowing!"

"Good, Lily. Just so you don't steal."

"Ha, ha," said the girl.

He headed to the easy chair and picked up the newspaper draped over the arm.

"Parallelogram," Sylvie whispered again, close to Claire's ear.

Claire didn't seem to be listening. She was doodling on the arithmetic paper while Lily checked her problems.

"You're messing up my homework," said Lily, looking over.

"Sorry."

"Those are funny-looking squares."

"Actually, they're called 'parallelograms.' You'll learn about them sometime."

"Fangl," Sylvie hissed into Claire's ear.

"I used to love geometry," said Claire. "I had

this funny old teacher. He was thin as a ruler."

Lily wasn't listening. She was trying to subtract a very small number from a very large one. "What, Mommy?"

"I was just remembering this teacher I once had."

Lily put down her pencil.

"We used to call him Fangl the Angle. I don't know why I'm thinking about him."

"Was he a good teacher?"

"Everybody made fun of him, but I kind of loved him."

That was all Sylvie could get out of Claire that night. She promised herself to try again tomorrow.

She did try the next night, and the one after the one after next; but although it was easy enough to get Claire to remember her old teacher, Sylvie couldn't get her to dream about him. He just hadn't made that deep an impression.

One night, when everyone was asleep, the girl

with the dark blue eyes took Sylvie out in the hallway. "Do you want to go home?"

Sylvie nodded.

"Come on."

Outside, the moon was high, and the donkey was still grazing. It shook its head and snorted.

"Aren't you coming?" Sylvie asked her friend.

"Can't. Claire has started remembering her dreams again, and she likes to see me in them."

"I like to see you, too."

"I'll find you."

"Promise?"

Sylvie climbed up, and the donkey plodded off, making right turn after right turn until at last it reached the edge of the city and headed into the mountains.

Part Four

THE CROSSING

chapter ten

Something was wrong. Sylvie couldn't say what it was, but she knew things were different as soon as she began her descent from the third southern mountain. Her father's new kingdom lay below her, looking glorious. Construction was still going on, most noticeably on the road into town, but that was to be expected. The trouble was elsewhere. She scanned the countryside. Shepherds' cottages and flocks of sheep dotted the high fields, glazed with late afternoon sun. Then there was the forest, and an occasional spiral of smoke from a woodcutter's hut. Over to the left was the high rocky ground where the thieves had their encampment. Beyond that, the road curved past the lake and led to the marketplace and the walls of the great castle itself.

That was it, she realized. The line of the castle was off. It wasn't obvious, but the west wall leaned inward slightly, instead of standing straight. The same with the east wall. The new parapet appeared tilted as well. *Keep your eye on the shape.* Fangl's words came back to her. Had the royal architect forgotten the original measurements? Were the masons using the wrong materials? Was she the only one who noticed?

As the donkey reached the valley, Sylvie noticed other changes. The flag was red and black instead of blue and white, and the people on the distant ramparts weren't waving to her, as they ordinarily would when a traveler approached.

She was now within hailing distance of the castle, but the drawbridge had not been lowered. Strange, she thought. Soon she was close enough to make out individual faces along the ramparts. She saw no sign of her parents, or even of the servants. And everyone was armed! She felt a chill as she recognized Hroth, the burliest of the thieves. He pulled an arrow from his quiver and notched it onto his bow.

Then a loud clanking and a rumbling sound announced the lowering of the drawbridge.

"Come on, little donkey," she cried, "let's get out of here!" She turned and jerked her heels against the donkey's sides, but by then the draw-bridge had thumped to the ground and a half dozen horsemen galloped across. They quickly overtook her.

"Let me alone, you oafs!" she shouted, but the riders simply encircled her and reined in their horses, preventing her from moving. Two of them, she realized, were Disappointed Ones she had rescued from the wilderness, but they didn't seem to recognize her. Seconds later, a seventh horseman raced from the castle, making the planks of the drawbridge rattle. It was Prince Riggeloff on Thunder.

"Welcome home, Princess," he said in his dark-edged voice. "Let me escort you to the king."

His words made no sense. What was he doing here, and why would he presume to escort her anywhere? She looked in his eyes, but they gave out no light. In the courtyard they all dismounted, and Sylvie was led into the great hallway, then down a torchlit corridor to the throne room. Two footmen swung opened the double doors while guards stood at attention on either side, their battle-axes gleaming. They were the same guards she'd always known, but they did not look at her. She took a breath and strode into the vaulted room. A long carpet made a blue pathway across the black stone floor.

"Pingree!" she gasped, looking to the distant throne.

The little man seemed to be swimming in a purple robe, and the crown sat low on his forehead. Seeing Sylvie, he stood and made a sweeping bow. Sylvie couldn't help thinking he looked like a frog in a basket of laundry.

"*King* Pingree," he corrected her. "At your service."

She came to within ten feet of him and stopped. "Where's my father?" she demanded.

He suppressed a giggle. "Out of sight, out of mind."

"You're out of *your* mind!" she shot back angrily. "Where is he?"

"Your tone, child, your tone. You're speaking to a king." This time the giggle did escape him.

"I don't see any king here. And what's so funny?"

"I was just thinking. Why did your father rule a *kingdom*?"

"What are you talking about?"

"Because he was such a *dumb king!*" Pingree rasped with laughter until he had to catch his breath.

"One thing hasn't changed," replied Sylvie. "You're still the least funny jester I've ever seen."

"Jester! I was never meant to be a jester."

"You admit it."

145

"I was meant for bigger things." He spread his arms wide and the crown slid down, covering his eyes.

"Or smaller crowns," she said dryly.

"Let's say we both have adjustments to make."

She looked at him steadily. Even his dull eye seemed bright, and his bright eye was brilliant. "Pingree, what have you done?"

"*King* Pingree. Lord and Master Pingree. Most Illustrious and Beloved Pingree. Gentle Pingree. Sweet, gentle Pingree."

She shook her head in disbelief.

"Well, we can work on all that," he said. "What have I done? I have changed the story line, that's what. And about time!"

"How?"

"The old Shawls of Slumber trick. I tossed them over the heads of the guards, then opened the gates to the prince and his men. A capital fellow, Prince Riggeloff."

"You stole that from the book!"

146

"My dear, I stole more than that."

"Who told you to do this, you toad?"

"Nobody! Isn't it glorious?" He whooped with laughter, and his eyes were dancing with secret lights. "I was a bad boy! I didn't do what I was told. I didn't say the lines that somebody— somebody without the slightest sense of humor— wrote for me years and years ago. I thought I'd go mad if I had to say those old jokes one more time."

"You *have* gone mad."

"Perhaps, but at least life is interesting. Admit it, Princess Sylvie. You have to admit our story is finally *interesting!*"

"I would like to see my father," said Sylvie.

"Sorry. Can't do that."

"What have you *done* with him?"

"Not a thing."

"If you'd done nothing, he would be here!"

"And yet he is not. A better man stands in his place."

"I see no man here."

"You'll see me differently soon."

"I want to see my father!"

"You will, you will, my dear. Some of his foolish subjects helped him run off into the forest, but when he learns that we have you, he'll come slinking back. He'll crawl in of his own free will."

"He escaped!"

"Yes, he escaped. Now even *he* is having an interesting story."

She felt the usual retorts rise inside her, indignant barbs that anyone in her situation would say. But she didn't say them. They weren't interesting. That word again. Instinct told her that if she wanted to save her father's kingdom, she'd have to come up with better dialogue.

"What's the matter?" Pingree taunted. "Troll got your tongue?"

"I was just thinking. Maybe you're right. The old story was getting a trifle—"

"Old?"

"Exactly."

"I knew it! I knew you were different!" He jumped up and did a little jig. "You couldn't stand the same routine any more than I could. You were always sneaking away to cross the eastern boundary. You don't know it, but I even followed you a couple of times."

"Did you really?"

"It's true! I couldn't *believe* the risks you were taking! That's when I decided that if I ever became king of this land"—he paused dramatically—"*when* I became king, I should say, I would choose you for my queen."

Sylvie's mouth opened, but no words came out. For once she found herself without a reply. "Did you really?" she said again.

"I've thought about it constantly. We think alike. We're both rebels. We're both smarter by a mile than anyone else around here. We're even the same size!"

Sylvie looked at the jester's spindly body. "We are, aren't we?" she said.

"What do you say?"

"I don't know," she said after a pause. "Do I have a choice?"

He cackled. "Now that you're out of that old book, you have no *end* of choices. Free will for all! That's Pingree's motto."

"Am I free?"

"Absolutely. Choose your own destiny! Be an individual!"

"Well, in that case . . ."

"Of course," he added with an arch in his left eyebrow, "you may not particularly *enjoy* the other choices."

"What are they?"

His bright eye glittered. "Actually, there's only one. Have you had a tour of our dungeon yet?"

"Not yet."

"You really should. I have a cell all picked out for you, right next to the one your parents will occupy."

"What if I still refuse you?"

"Oh, you really *haven't* seen the dungeon!"

"I see," she said slowly. "You're very persuasive. In fact, I don't think I've ever heard marriage proposed in such an irresistible way before."

"It's true," he said, hanging his head modestly. "I am irresistible."

"Completely. But could I think this over a little while?"

"Sure! Take your time. I'll come to you later for your answer. Shall we say midnight?"

"Thank you." She nodded a fraction.

"Thank you what?"

"Excuse me?"

"I said, thank you *what?*"

"Thank you—Your Highness?" She gave a half curtsy.

He jumped up with a laugh and ran right around the throne, screaming, "Yes! Yes! I knew it!"

After a solitary dinner of frogs' legs and cabbage in the great dining hall, Princess Sylvie was

151

shown to her old bedchamber at the top of the west turret. It turned out the chambermaids had been sleeping there during her absence and had left it a mess. Without anyone to direct them, they'd stopped making beds or emptying trash bins. They had taken Pingree's motto to heart: Free will for all. Sylvie brushed cake crumbs off the coverlet and watched as a rat darted from the corner and seized a morsel. It sat on its haunches nibbling, quite unafraid.

She'd never noticed that large rat hole before. Then she realized the walls were separated at the corners. The room no longer had right angles, but tilted like a trapezoid. When it was nearly midnight, Sylvie went to the window, then climbed out onto the balcony to see better. It was a brilliant night, with all the stars in their places and a half-moon rising. That's the way her own world had been in the days when she lived between the comforting covers of a book. The plot had been clear as a constellation.

She thought of Pingree and shivered. Marry

that creature? She would be his queen, he had said. But queen of what? What was left of the kingdom? Her friend with the dark blue eyes was right: The story was falling apart. Sylvie looked up at the constellation of Orion, brilliant as white fire. "Help me," she said deep inside herself. "Help me to help my father."

A clumping of booted feet stopped outside her chamber. Then the door burst open, and three soldiers barged in. "Where is she?" came Pingree's voice from the hall. The little man appeared in the doorway, his purple robe dragging along the floor.

"I'm out here, Your Highness," called Sylvie.

"Ah!" he said. "How romantic."

She hopped up on the railing. "Don't come any closer, please."

"Stop her!"

The soldiers started toward the balcony as Sylvie teetered precariously.

"Wait!" Pingree cried in an agony of indecision. The soldiers paused. It was clear they could

153

not reach her in time, if she had it in her mind to do something foolish. "Don't move, anybody!" he shouted.

The word "interesting" came to Sylvie's mind again. The darkened kingdom lay reeling below her while above the heavens sparkled. All that held her suspended between them was her sense of balance. If only this were a book, she thought, there would be a handy vine she could swing away on, but there were no vines on this brand-new castle, and she was making up the story as she went along.

The castle roof was just above her room, she realized. If she could get up there, they'd never catch her. The rough-hewn stones on the outer wall might give her enough surface to grab on to. What alternative did she have? Pingree would hold her hostage until her father gave himself up. And King Walther *would* give up.

"Don't!" shrilled the jester.

She stood on her tiptoes, swaying. She heard

154

the clumping of the soldiers' boots as they raced to stop her, then a different, faster thumping sound she didn't recognize.

"Don't!"

But she had already swung herself away from the balcony and was clinging to the outside stones, struggling to get a footing. She found a good grip and was able to take a step higher. The first soldier reached the window and had begun clambering out, but Sylvie couldn't rush what she was doing.

A second step, higher and farther from the window. She could hear the man grunting as he climbed up on the railing, trying to reach her.

A third step. Soon she'd be beyond his grasp. The strange muffled thumping she'd heard seemed closer than before. Was it her heart?

Another step. She felt the tips of the soldier's fingers touching her ankle, straining to get hold of her. No! she shouted inside her head. But her weight was on that foot, and she couldn't move it until she found the next foothold.

The hand encircled her ankle. She tried to kick him away with her other foot, but then the man yanked and Sylvie felt a terrified emptiness in her stomach as she started to fall away from the building, her arms windmilling. Suddenly, she was hurtling downward, with the thumping sound louder than ever in her ears.

A moment later something heavy slammed against her body, ripping into the heavy material of the cape, and then she wasn't falling anymore.

"Owl!" she cried. "Dear, dear owl!"

The great bird gripped her with crooked claws and beat its wings violently to carry her weight. At first they lost altitude, dropping lower and lower till they skimmed the treetops. A high branch struck Sylvie's foot and knocked off a shoe.

"You can do it!" she cried.

Careening onward, Sylvie managed a quick glance behind her. Soldiers were running about on the ramparts. A volley of arrows sailed out through the darkness. And there, in the distance, was the west turret where she'd been standing a few seconds ago. In the lighted window stood Pingree, a small black silhouette, his arms raised in fury.

chapter eleven

What struck Sylvie first, when she caught sight of her parents hurrying toward her through the trees, was her mother's dirty face. Somehow that touched her, as did her mother's cry of pleasure as they fell into each other's arms. This was not the proper, imperious queen Sylvie had known, but a woman who had been through trouble and whose joy at seeing her daughter was so keen it seemed a kind of pain.

The king joined in a three-way hug from which they all emerged with tears in their eyes.

"We'll get you back on your thrones," Sylvie said fiercely.

Her father nodded. "I know. Stories always turn out in the end."

"What happened to your shoe?" said the queen, blowing her nose.

"Long story," said Sylvie. "But I have good news. Claire remembers us again."

"Do you think," said the queen, "she'll call us back to be in her dreams? I do like living in a town."

"It's possible."

"Princess?" It was Fangl, the geometry teacher. The rust spot on his head had spread to one cheek, like a terrible disease. "I don't suppose you were able to bring up my name."

"I did bring up your name, Fangl, and Claire remembers you well."

"Really!" His face brightened. Even the rusty patches glowed. "Any chance she might need me for a dream?"

"I don't see why not."

It was possible, of course, but it kept not happening. The longer it didn't happen, the less often anyone mentioned it. The king and his people would just have to make the best of their time in

159

the wilderness. A number of servants loyal to the king still lived in the castle, and they secretly brought food, beauty supplies for the queen, building materials, even some weapons. The weapons made possible occasional nighttime raids, but King Walther simply didn't have enough men to retake the castle. Nor was the jester—even with Prince Riggeloff as his Minister of War—able to hunt down and capture the king.

No one could say how long these skirmishes went on—the fruitless racing about in the woods, the flinging of spears, the creeping through castle corridors. Meanwhile, Pingree the Pretender remained on the throne. During this period, Sylvie watched helplessly as the reddish patches spread to various parts of Fangl's body. What was the matter with Claire? Why didn't she *dream* about him? At least, she thought, the royal family had been spared the disease.

Finally the day came when the castle's sentry

spotted a dark figure descending the mountain and sang out, "Stranger coming!" Even in the forest, the king's followers stopped and listened to the distant trumpets braying. From her lookout on the rocky point, Sylvie could see the crowds form on the distant battlements and hear Riggeloff shout, "Move aside!" as he strapped on his sword. Hroth, Thomas, and the others began lifting their long bows.

But the rider did not take the road to the castle, turning instead onto the forest path that led to King Walther's encampment. Sylvie raced to the clearing. "It's you!" she cried as the girl with the dark blue eyes dismounted.

King Walther came forward, leaning heavily on his cane, and Queen Emmeline followed, holding out her royal hand for the girl to kiss. As before, there was a celebration, with feasting and dancing and storytelling, but the girl seemed quieter than she'd been the last time. Toward the end of the festivities, she asked King Walther if she could speak to him and the queen and Sylvie in private.

As always, she used the simplest words. What would they think of leaving this place and rebuilding in another land?

"But we're fighting to regain the castle!" the king sputtered. "We can't leave Pingree the Pretender in control!"

The girl nodded. "How are you feeling these days, sire?"

"Me? Sound as a drum. Oh this, you mean!" He waved the cane in the air. "A touch of sciatica. I'm not as young as I was."

"Excuse me for saying it, sire, but you are *exactly* as young as you were. Fictional characters don't get older."

Sylvie looked at her father. "She's right!"

"It's nothing."

"A reddish patch on your hip?" said Sylvie's young friend.

"Probably something I ate."

"And you, Queen Emmeline. How have you been?"

"Perfect, as you can see."

"You're using more makeup above your right cheek."

"Have you come to insult us?"

"I have come to save you, if I can."

"How?" cried Sylvie, who'd been looking at her parents with distress. "We'll do anything."

"Things are not the same in the outside world," said the girl. "Claire is no longer young, and she is no longer well."

Sylvie caught her breath. "I have to go to her!"

"Of course."

"This is terrible," said the king. He went to the window, then came back, chewing on the edge of his mustache. "What can we do?"

"Nothing for Claire, but something for yourselves."

"But," he said, "isn't it true that we could go on living here as before?"

163

"Perhaps."

"Didn't you say that once a character has been dreamed, he will live forever?"

"In a way."

"Well, what *did* you mean?"

"A character, once dreamed, will live as long as the dreamer lives."

A silence settled over everyone.

"Of course, I don't know for sure," the girl went on. "Nobody really knows."

"I see." The king continued chewing on his mustache. "Where would we go?"

"You are fortunate. Claire has a daughter named Lily, who has dreamed about your story. Not in recent years, but that may not matter. It could still be possible for you and your people to cross over."

"What do you mean, 'cross over'?"

"Move from the mind of Claire into the mind of her daughter."

"That sounds impossible!"

"It may be."

"How would we do it?"

"By entering the daughter's dreams."

"But, my dear, we've never *met* this child."

"She is not a child anymore, and she knows your story by heart."

The king was silent. He didn't notice the tears filling Sylvie's eyes. First, her little friend Claire puts on this strange grown-up disguise; then she gets old and sick. And what about Sylvie's own parents? If her friend was right, they had caught the same disease that was eating away Fangl! How long could they stay out here in the wilderness before they rusted away completely?

The king stood up. "We will think about these things and give you our answer in the morning. Thank you, my dear, for telling us."

The royal party returned to the celebration, but the king's heart wasn't in it, and he and the queen retired early. Sylvie's young friend was shown to a special tent furnished with large blue pillows and a view of the distant castle.

After saying good night, Sylvie passed her parents' tent, where she heard her mother and father talking in low tones. Later, with the flap of her tent tied open, she lay awake watching the stars hanging like a basket of lights above the mountain. Her stomach didn't feel very well, but she knew it was nerves. This new adventure she was about to set out on didn't feel like a beginning, it felt like the end of everything she treasured. Watching a gray moth flapping in confused circles above her, Sylvie wondered if this was the last night she'd lie in her own bed, in her father's kingdom.

Claire's kingdom, really, she reminded herself. At least it was on Claire's land. She remembered how helpless Claire had been during that first adventure they'd had together in the Muddy Forest. She couldn't even climb the tree without Sylvie's help. But she was the sort of person you *wanted* to give a lift to.

At midnight, Sylvie heard a soft whisper outside the door. "Princess, are you awake?"

It was Fangl. Sylvie jumped from bed and went out to meet him.

"You want me to speak to Claire again?" Sylvie asked, strolling with him toward the rocky point.

"Yes, but not about me. I don't matter anymore."

"You matter tremendously!"

They passed through a dark glade that led to an outcropping of rock.

"The *kingdom* matters," Fangl went on. "Listen. I've made some measurements, and I can tell you the king will not regain his throne the way he's going about it."

"I know."

"He is inside the problem."

"I'm not sure what that means."

"You can't solve a problem from inside it."

"What, then?"

"You've got to get outside—outside the parallelogram."

"Too much geometry, Fangl. Just tell me what you mean."

"I mean, Princess, that you're the only one who can save the kingdom, because you're the only one who can leave it."

They reached the highest point of land and looked out over the dark valley.

"I don't understand," said the princess. "I have to leave it to save it?"

"Exactly." Fangl pointed toward the castle in the distance. "Otherwise, you get this."

"Yes, I've noticed there's something wrong with the castle walls."

"They're going to collapse."

"What's the matter? Were they measured wrong?"

"I checked that. They used the wrong materials. All the builders knew about was book glue."

"The castle was stuck together with *glue*?" said Sylvie.

"That's fine as long as you're in a book. But it doesn't work out here."

168

It was all too much for her. "I don't understand!" she said, tears starting in her eyes. "How can I solve anything when I'm out in Claire's world? What does she know about building castles? What good will it do my parents if I manage to cross into somebody else's mind?"

"I don't have the figures on that. All I know is that we'll all die if you stay here. And your story will die, too."

"That can't happen."

"It wouldn't be the first time. The wilderness is littered with forgotten stories that will never be retold."

Sylvie looked at his thin, kindly face and knew, in a way she had not known before, that she had no choice. She held the old tutor's hand. The back of it was rough and dark. She lifted it to her lips and kissed it.

chapter twelve

Sylvie woke to the bonging of the council bell. From her tent she could see peasants, knights, and servants filing into the clearing. She dressed hurriedly.

"Need any help?" Her friend with the dark blue eyes was peering in the tent flap.

"I can't get my braids right," said Sylvie.

The girl looked surprised. "I always visualized you wearing combs."

"Can't. They keep coming out."

"I should have thought of that. Sorry."

"Sorry for what?"

She shook her head. "Not important. Here. Let me." The girl stood behind Sylvie and quickly twisted her hair into perfect braids.

Sylvie's father and mother were waiting for the girls when they came out. Then they went together to greet their subjects.

The king raised his arms for silence. "We have lived many years in our new kingdom," he began. "With our own hands we built it from the stones and trees of this mountainside. All of us together have done this, and until recently we lived here happily."

He looked darkly toward the edge of the crowd where Hroth and Riggeloff stood with their hands resting on their sword hilts.

"I have asked representatives from the castle to be here. You all know Prince Riggeloff and Hroth."

The crowd began whispering. Someone hissed.

"I have not forgotten their treachery, but we have come to a moment of decision, and they need to be part of it."

Then he told the news. He spoke of the

prophecy that they would all live as long as the dreamer lived whose land this was. He said that no one knew what would happen if the dreamer died. Perhaps they would all disappear, like mist rising from a lake. They might rust slowly away, as they'd seen others do. Or they might live on. They had a chance now to move to another land and start over. He could not make that decision for them. If they voted to leave, he and his family would go with them. If they chose to stay and take their chances, he and the queen would remain, although Princess Sylvie would probably make the attempt to cross over to the mind of Claire's daughter, Lily.

The crowd was silent. Some of them looked curiously at Sylvie's mysterious friend with the dark blue eyes. Not all of the stares were friendly.

"Excuse me, sire, for asking," said the chief gamekeeper. "Who is this outsider who seems to have so much influence over you?"

The king was clearly surprised by the question.

"She is a great friend of the princess's and of ourselves," he said solemnly. "We trust her completely."

"Is she the one who says we got to move," called out the royal cook, "and go off who knows where?"

"Who is she, anyway?" called out the woodcutter, shaking a gnarled stick in the air.

The king shot a worried look at the girl. "I believe," he said, "that this dear girl was the very first Reader of our book."

That caused more hubbub than ever.

"If she's a Reader," called the goatherd, "what's she doing inside the story?"

"We aren't *in* a book!" shouted the woodcutter.

"That's right!" called the man's round-cheeked wife. "We're out in the back end of nowhere, and it's her fault!"

Arguments and accusations broke out until the king raised his arms and his chief councillor shouted, "Silence!"

When everyone was quiet, the girl with the dark blue eyes stepped forward. "Hello, everybody," she said quite calmly. "It sounds as if you all like where you are."

"What would you know?" challenged a peasant's wife.

"We don't need outsiders telling us!" shouted another.

The girl looked out over the crowd and waited. "I certainly don't blame you for wanting to stay. I think you *should* stay."

"Hear, hear," said the usual group of soldiers.

"As long as you don't mind having a jester on the throne."

Murmurs rose from the crowd.

"And the castle about to collapse."

"It's true!" shouted the goatherd. "Look how crooked it is!" Others began pointing and talking.

"And the whole place likely to evaporate at any moment," she continued.

"She may be right, you know," said the youngest lady-in-waiting.

174

"Or wrong," replied the girl with the dark blue eyes. "Nobody knows what will happen. That's why your king"——she turned and looked at King Walther——"your gracious, wise king," she added, "has consented to let you make your own decision."

"Hear, hear!"

"I think," she added, "that's more than the jester would do for you."

"Good point!" said the goatherd.

"It's up to us, then?" called a voice.

"That's what your king is telling you," said the girl. "Let his wisdom, and your own, be your guide." She stepped back and gave Sylvie's hand a brief squeeze.

"You were wonderful!" Sylvie whispered.

"I'm good at words," said the girl simply.

People began talking among themselves. A number glanced around at the mountains and the bird-bannered sky beyond. They gazed at the king and at one another as if for the first, or the last, time. Several people spoke. A herdsman wanted to know if they could bring their animals with them. Only a few, said the king.

Riggeloff asked if King Walther was sure they would even be *able* to cross over to Claire's daughter, a person none of them except Sylvie had ever seen.

"I am not sure at all."

"In that case," declared Riggeloff, "I vote to stay in the kingdom we have built, where my men and I have robbed so many people so enjoyably, and where we now hold the upper hand."

"Aye," one of the king's knights spoke up, "I, too, would stay until we've thrown the jester from the castle window and punished Riggeloff's men for their cowardly attacks."

"Hear, hear!"

"We shall see who's cowardly!" roared Riggeloff.

"Enough!" shouted the king.

"But what if we disappear?" the youngest lady-in-waiting said in a quavery voice.

"That's as likely to happen if we leave as if we stay," replied Queen Emmeline, finally entering the debate. It was clear what *she* would prefer.

In the end, the people voted to remain in the valley, with the understanding that Sylvie was going to try to make the crossing. The king was gratified. He didn't want to start over, and neither did the queen. They never had been adventurous. Kings and queens like to have solid thrones beneath them and stone walls around them, and they still had hopes of retaking the castle.

And so preparations were begun for Sylvie's journey. Her mother wanted to provide her with a caravan and quantities of provisions, from baby onions to wren's eggs, and she grieved that she no longer had the resources to do it. Sylvie ended up taking her locket, a wedge of cheese, a fresh, warm loaf of bread, a single change of clothing, and—just in case—the wonderful invisible fish, dried off, rolled up, and thrust in her bag. Her young friend, who had brought nothing except the cloak she was wearing, mounted the donkey while the princess hugged her parents good-bye.

Sylvie had a sudden fear that she might not see her family again, and she looked at them with a tender intensity, as if to memorize everything, from her mother's smile lines to her father's upturned mustache, quivering just now with emotion. Maybe she should stay after all. She had good ideas. Surely she could come up with a way to regain the castle from the Pretender. Glancing over at the distant walls, she found her attention caught by a brief glint on the west turret. It was the jester, and for a moment she thought she was seeing the reflection of his brilliant eye catching the sun. Then she realized he was looking at her through a spyglass, matching her stare for stare. She felt the anger well up inside her.

But then she caught sight of Fangl at the edge of the crowd, nodding at her encouragingly, and she remembered: *You can't solve a problem from inside it.* She sighed. It was clear what she had to do. Flashing a brave smile at her parents, she climbed on the donkey behind her friend and started off.

No sooner were they out of sight of the castle than the city rose up before them, the gleaming buildings far taller now than before. They took the same left turn, then left, left, left, left, left, and left, until they came to the dark Victorian house bathed in moonlight. The girls hurried inside and up the stairs to Claire's waking mind.

But there was no sign of Claire. Instead, a heavy old woman lay propped on pillows in the canopied bed.

"Shh," whispered the girl with the dark blue eyes, "she's sleeping."

Sylvie's eyes widened, realizing who lay before them. "My goodness!" she said. "Is that Claire?"

"Your little friend, Claire, yes."

Sylvie felt her throat tightening. "Do all Readers change around like this?"

Her friend nodded solemnly. "They start

179

little, then they get big, then they disappear."

"What do you mean—disappear?" She felt her throat tightening even more.

The girl with the dark blue eyes laid a hand gently on Sylvie's wrist.

"No!" whispered Sylvie angrily.

A nurse came rattling in with medicines. She gazed at the patient, then left the tray on the night table.

"Here," whispered Sylvie's friend. "Let's sit in the corner."

Sylvie followed her friend to a tapestry-covered ottoman. By her feet she placed the bag with her extra clothes and the rolled-up fish.

After a little while, a man entered quietly and pulled up a chair by the bed. He was tall with thinning hair and soft-looking brown eyes. "Claire," he said.

She stirred.

"Time for your medicine."

"Oh," she said, opening her eyes. "Hello, you."

They talked together quietly of people Sylvie knew nothing about, and then Claire took several pills with water and lay back on the pillows. The man was leaning forward to kiss her when a thump of footsteps made him look toward the door. A heavyset man entered briskly, holding a flame-colored bouquet. Tufts of reddish hair stood up on either side of his bald head.

"How nice, Richard," said Claire. "Tom, can you take the flowers?"

"So! How's the patient doing?" said the bald man. His voice made the spoon on the medicine tray quiver.

"Tom is taking good care of me."

"Thought any more about the matter we were discussing?"

Sylvie was trying to make sense of this from her seat in the corner. "That big one. Do I know him?"

"You should."

It was soon evident that the large man wasn't happy with the way the conversation was going. He couldn't sit still, but kept readjusting his body in the smallish chair. He was talking about papers and signatures and envelopes marked PAST DUE. In the middle of it Claire's eyes closed. His voice trailed off. "Rest yourself," he said, hoisting himself to his feet. "We'll talk tomorrow."

By the door, he took out a cigarette and snapped open his lighter. Sylvie watched the glow of the flame as he bent his head toward it, and suddenly, against her will, she remembered everything. She was again seeing the terrible firestick coming closer and closer, and behind it the pudgy cheeks of a boy named Ricky.

Sylvie stared.

"Just be sure," whispered the girl with the dark blue eyes, "that you don't end up in *his* dreams."

chapter thirteen

Ricky's footsteps boomed down the staircase, then Tom clapped his hands on his knees and stood up. "Well," he said, "I'd better get these in water." He headed to the kitchen.

Sylvie's friend whispered, "Go over and ask to see Lily."

"Who?"

"Her daughter."

Sylvie left her bag by the ottoman and approached the bed. "It's me."

Claire's eyes were closed, but a smile started along her lips.

"Would you like to hear our story again?"

Slowly the woman nodded.

"Maybe your daughter could tell it?"

Just then the man came back with a vase filled with the extravagant flowers. "Ah, you're awake."

"Tom. Call Lily, would you? Ask if she can come."

"She's planning to fly in next week, remember?"

"See if she can get an earlier flight."

Tom looked at her a long moment. Sylvie watched him. She had never seen such tortured tenderness on a human face. "Of course," he said.

He went to call, and Sylvie turned to her friend. "Fly?" she said. "Readers can fly?"

"It's an expression."

Sylvie was relieved. Readers were entirely too alarming as it was, changing shapes and ages right and left.

A few hours later, a slender young woman in a tailored skirt hurried in. Her long brown hair was stylishly cut, but needed a comb. She went immediately to the bed.

"Lily," said Claire, her face softening at the sight of her.

"Dad scared me half to death. He said to drop everything."

"That's Tom for you."

"You've got to train him not to frighten people."

"Too late."

"Hello, daughter!" Claire's husband came in and scooped Lily into a hug. "How about some hot chocolate?"

"Please."

Lily and her mother talked while Tom came and went, fetching their drinks, bringing the mail, looking for pillows. Once he bumped into the nurse as she was rounding the corner with a glass of water.

"Tom, don't *hover!*" said Claire.

When he finally left, Claire shook her head. "He's the one I worry about. I don't think he'll know what to do."

"Neither will I."

"Oh, you'll be fine. You've got your writing. You're getting married. You're strong."

"I don't feel very strong."

"But you are."

The young woman sighed.

Claire paused, as if gathering her meager reserves of strength. "Have you had any luck in your search?" she said.

"Noooo," said Lily, giving the word a pained little twist. "And I wanted *so* much to bring you a copy."

"Couldn't you find it?" Claire laid her head back on the pillow.

"I tried the rare bookshops. I tried the libraries. Finally I wrote to the Library of Congress. It sure would help if you knew the author's name."

"I don't think there was a name. I'm almost sure there wasn't."

Lily shook her head. "Mysterious. It's as though it didn't exist."

"But it did. It does."

"Do you think it could have been privately

printed? Sometimes people do that. Just a few copies for friends."

"I don't know."

"Did your grandmother ever say where she got it?"

Claire shook her head. "She just said it was a gift. Something she'd been given when she was young."

"It was such a cozy story."

"Remember when we used to curl up in this bed, and you'd ask me to tell it to you over and over?"

"It was my favorite story in the world," Lily replied.

"Well. . . . Do you think you could, this time, tell it to *me*?"

Sitting in the corner, Sylvie felt a light hand touch hers. "It's time," whispered the girl with the dark blue eyes.

"Really?" Sylvie reached down for her bag, but her friend shook her head.

"No, not to cross over. To help her."

187

"I don't think I can still remember it," Claire's daughter was saying.

"You'll remember," said Claire.

"Well, I know the general story, of course. But..."

Claire's eyes closed. "Tell."

Sylvie looked at Lily. She saw the pain in her eyes, and the fear that she would fail. Sylvie moved closer. She wanted to reach out and stroke her hair, but was afraid to scare her. Instead, she murmured the opening lines of *The Great Good Thing*.

The young woman's face eased into a smile, and she began to speak the words aloud.

"Yes," Claire murmured, her eyes still closed. "Keep going."

With Sylvie's prompting, Lily went on, helping the giant tortoise, rescuing the blind owl, leaping into the Mere, finding the Cave of Diamonds, turning the thieves into crickets, on and on to the end. Claire had long since drifted into sleep. Her daughter was exhausted, but pleased and amazed. She had remembered every word!

Sylvie was exhausted as well. This girl Lily had no way of knowing how much was depending on her. Upon her slim shoulders rode the fate of Sylvie and her parents, the kingdom, the story itself. She seemed nice enough, but was she up to it?

"Can you stay awhile?" Tom asked in his don't-wake-your-mama voice. He handed Lily a fresh mug of hot chocolate with two marshmallows.

"I've cleared the next three days." She sat on the edge of the bed, holding the mug by her face to feel the steam against her eyelids.

"Your old room is ready for you," he said.

Lily looked up with tear-glazed eyes.

After Lily had left, Princess Sylvie and her friend went quietly to the bedside. It was hard to recognize in the gray-haired woman before them the excited playmate Sylvie had loved so well.

"She was my favorite," said the girl with the dark blue eyes.

Sylvie nodded.

"She was the only one I could entrust the book to."

"She loved that book," Sylvie said simply.

"She did, didn't she?" The girl was thoughtful. "She never believed she could do a Great Good Thing, but she did any number of them. She let you into her dreams. She kept the story alive."

"And she was kind," said Sylvie.

"Yes. She did me a great kindness when I was dying."

"I remember."

"She read to me. Even when she thought I couldn't hear her, she read from our book."

"Could you really hear her?"

"Every word."

They stood watching awhile longer, then quietly slipped out of the room.

That night Sylvie and her friend waited by the daughter's bedside while she slept. But although

Lily had several dreams, one of them quite frightening, they weren't right for Sylvie to enter. She'd have to try again tomorrow night.

The next day took forever to get through. Claire's brother came by with an attaché case and a pen, but Claire wasn't up to signing anything. She seemed weaker than before. Twice she asked to hear the story again, and twice her daughter began it. Both times Claire fell asleep after a few minutes.

That evening while her mother slept, Lily sat up talking with her father about the future and how they should handle Uncle Richard's business schemes. Princess Sylvie had no idea what they were talking about, but her friend listened intently. Of course she'd be interested, Sylvie realized, remembering that the girl was in fact Claire's grandmother and used to own this house.

After everyone had gone to bed, Sylvie asked, "What's a second mortgage?"

The girl shook her head as if to dispel a dream.

"It's nothing. I can't tell you how much more I like your story than this one we're watching."

"Really?"

"Oh, yes. Yours is about treasure. This one's about money. There is all the difference in the world between treasure and money."

Later that night they slipped into the room where Claire's daughter was sleeping. Her dream did not look like fun. Four black dogs were tearing a rabbit to pieces. Then the animals caught sight of a young girl and snarled. She turned and ran, and the dogs raced after her through crowded streets. Sylvie sat in a big chair across the room, waiting for the dream to be over. In her hand she gripped the rolled-up fish.

Finally, the terrified child came to the end of a street. A filthy river lay before her, and beyond that, on the far side, the white turret of a castle. Sylvie sat up. She recognized the distant country as her own kingdom.

"When do you think we can go in?" she whispered to her friend.

192

"You have the fish? I think you should unroll him."

"All right." She quickly undid the string around the crinkly fish. "I'm ready."

Just then, one of the dogs lunged at the girl, and she screamed and fell off the end of the pier into the swirling water.

"This is it!" said Sylvie. "Let's go!"

Her friend did not move.

"Come on!" Sylvie repeated. "I don't think that girl can swim!"

"You go ahead, dear."

"What?" She looked over at her and was stunned to see an elderly lady with stooped shoulders draped in a shawl.

"I can't go with you," said the old woman. "This girl has never dreamed of me. But she has dreamed about your story and is about to again."

"No!" cried Sylvie. "Don't scare me! Take off that disguise."

"I can't. Under this disguise is another disguise."

"No!"

"The girl with the dark blue eyes is a disguise."

"I need you!"

The woman smiled, and in that smile Sylvie recognized her friend who had seen her through so many adventures. "You'll always have me," she replied. "But right now I have to stay with Claire. In fact, she's about to have a dream about me. Her very last."

"What?"

"Don't you worry. Hurry along. You don't want that girl to drown." She gave Sylvie a quick kiss on the forehead.

Sylvie looked from the old woman to the girl thrashing in the water. "Promise you'll find me?"

"We'll find each other."

"Promise!"

"I promise. Go!"

Sylvie ran to the end of the pier. A cold wind whipped her hair, and the unrolled fish flapped like a flag. She paused only a moment.

Part Five

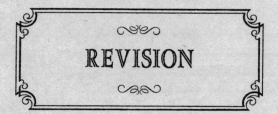

REVISION

chapter fourteen

Sylvie was delighted with the new country. Lily's mind was much more orderly than Claire's had been. You didn't suddenly trip over yellow-eyed pythons or splash through ponds that a moment ago were windows. If you wanted pythons, you went to the Reptile House. If you wanted ponds, you went to the Water Resource Center, which contained bodies of water of all sizes, each marked with a small, hand-lettered sign. Lily was clearly a girl who knew what she was about.

Of course, there was the occasional nightmare, such as the one that had gotten Sylvie here in the first place. Such dreams did not happen often, but when they did it was best to keep your head down until they blew over and the dogs were recaptured.

Several of the dreams were not frightening so much as sad. In one, Lily was cleaning out a basement strewn with wilted and rotting marigolds. Sylvie, who had no role in this dream, watched as Lily swept the piles of flowers into large metal containers. The smell was sour, and the basement dank. Then Lily's father came in and stood watching. "Lily," he said in his softest voice. "Your mother wanted me to tell you that she's all right."

With a little cry, Lily ran into her father's arms. "Really? She's all right?"

After the dream was over and Sylvie was on her own, she realized that Claire might or might not be all right, but she had definitely died—whatever that meant. It was something that Readers did. Personally, Sylvie didn't see the point of it. In her story, the villains might be turned into crickets and eaten by the owl, but they were fine again when the next Reader opened the book.

Lily was a writer, Sylvie learned, but not a successful one, to judge by the blizzard of rejection slips that whizzed past the window during one dream. Here was a person who could organize a story as easily as she could organize her ribbon drawer, and yet slip after printed slip said that her work did not "meet our current needs."

Many of Lily's dreams had to do with successes: a piano concert ending in wild applause, or a trek up an icy mountainside to rescue an attractive young man. Sylvie appeared regularly in these stories. Naturally, Lily appeared as well, sometimes as a twelve-year-old, at other times as the sensible twenty-three-year-old she, in fact, was.

But something was missing, for both of them. Sylvie was the only member of her original story to make the crossing, and she longed to see her family, even her enemies. What, she wondered, was that creature Pingree up to? And she *fiercely* missed the girl with the dark blue eyes. Sometimes she'd linger in the Water Resource Center looking for a body of water that looked like the Mere of Remind. She'd take out the golden locket and see what image showed up this time. Once she wept to see a picture of her father leaning on *two* canes! Part of his face was in shadow. At least Sylvie hoped it was shadow. "Father! How can I help you? What am I *doing* here?"

Once upon a time she had felt trapped inside her story with its familiar characters and predictable plot. Now she felt locked *out* of it. She didn't even have a castle to live in, just several connecting rooms high up in a steel building.

Lily, on her part, was suffering because she hadn't made a name for herself as an author. Sylvie looked at her and said the first thing that came to mind: "Maybe you should let more of your animals out."

"I know I should. But I'm afraid of them."

From what she had seen of Lily's nightmares, Sylvie couldn't blame her. But later she had an idea. She discounted it at first, but it returned. Soon the idea grew into a wonderful hope.

One evening, toward the end of a pleasant but not very dramatic dream, the two of them were walking across a deserted parade ground. Sylvie decided now was the time to bring up her idea. "You're a good writer," she said.

"Can you get a publisher to say that?"

"Maybe you're writing the wrong thing."

"I write what I know about."

"Do you?"

"Sure. Relationships. Office politics."

"Listen to me. You're supposed to listen to voices you hear in dreams. I say you can do better than office—whatever it is you said."

"You think so?"

"I know what you should write. Remember this when you wake up. Will you remember this?"

"I'll remember."

"I have to ask you three times in a dream for you to remember once."

"I'll remember. What is it?"

"You should write a book. It's called *The Great Good Thing*."

Her friend's eyes widened with excitement, then dimmed with doubt. "But it isn't my story."

"No, it's *my* story. I am lonely for my story."

"Are you? Of course you must be."

"I think the world is lonely for my story."

Her friend was silent.

"What's the matter?"

The girl gave a pretty frown. "Well, it wouldn't be, you know, original, would it?"

"For heaven's sake!" Sylvie cried, finally losing patience. "Would you stop worrying about being an author for once and just write!"

The girl stared at Sylvie. She'd never seen her like this. "Well," she said, "maybe I could do something. Would you help me?"

Revision

"I'll help, I'll help, don't worry!"

The young woman walked along a little farther, then turned and gave Sylvie a sideways look that was almost sly. *"Really?"*

Sylvie went over and gave her a hug. While she was at it, she stepped hard on her foot to make her wake up right away.

chapter fifteen

Over the next four months, with Sylvie's prompting, Lily wrote furiously. Her husband was not pleased. Up till now, his young wife had worked on her writing from six until seven-thirty in the morning (when she brought him his coffee), and from one to two-thirty in the afternoon. Now he found himself having to get his own coffee, and sometimes dinner as well.

Princess Sylvie was just as busy. She could hear Lily's thoughts all around her and the computer keys clicking, and she constantly had to keep Lily from putting in adjectives and little improvements of her own. "Just say what happened!" Sylvie would call out.

"Oh, leave me alone!" the writer's voice would answer, but then she'd end up taking out the extra words, most of them, anyway.

At times Sylvie was guilty of putting in extra words herself. She realized she had no choice, if she was ever to be happy again.

"I don't remember this stuff," the writer's voice echoed overhead as Sylvie dictated the new material.

"Trust me!" Sylvie called back.

Lily grumbled, but wrote what she was told. When it was finished, she read the story aloud in front of the mirror while Sylvie listened, stopping her to make corrections. At last the book was ready, complete with a short preface explaining that this was "a story my mother used to tell me every night at bedtime, when I was a girl. She said it was from a book that had come to her grandmother as a gift early in the last century. Although no copy has yet turned up, the story is indeed a gift, and I'm retelling it in hopes it will not be lost again."

Then the manuscript was gone. Off in the mail somewhere. It was gone for a very long time.

At last the morning came when Sylvie opened her eyes and heard the sound of unfamiliar birds. She couldn't tell at first what was different, but a feeling of excitement crept over her. She realized she was not in a high-rise hotel anymore, but in something very much like a castle. Jumping up, she ran to look out the arched stone window. Far below her lay a colorful countryside, too colorful for eyes that had become used to shifting shapes and the dim-lit hours between dreams. Sylvie kept expecting the scene to change, as it always did if you looked at it steadily. But it was just there, like a picture in a book. It didn't turn into a golf course or the Home Furnishings section of a big department store. It was an empty picture, though. Not a soul in sight.

A distant sound reached her, and she strained

to hear. Drums, and yes, the tinny bleat of far-off trumpets. She climbed out the window onto the stone balcony, but could see nothing. Then she thought she detected a faint glimmer in the morning light. Gradually it grew, and she made out little banners and horses, and in the front of them jugglers and tumblers and musicians.

"Oh, my goodness!" she cried, racing down the circular staircase. Down and down she went, all the way to the courtyard, then across the draw-bridge into the wide avenue. Yes, she could see them clearly, a multitude, much closer now, shouting and talking while bugles tooted and drums banged busily away.

There was her father at the front of the procession, his armor gleaming, and beside him her mother the queen carrying her lively lapdog. Just behind them came the chief councillor and then the courtiers and a whole flock of ladies. Farther back rode Prince Riggeloff and his men, then the peasants and townspeople with their wagons and animals. Sylvie let out a yip of joy and ran up the road to meet them. When her parents saw Sylvie, they called out and waved merrily.

"No cane, Father?" she said after he'd dismounted and given her a paternal hug.

"Cane? Why would I have a cane?"

She was about to ask him more when the queen's lapdog started yipping, then jumped down and raced off after a marmalade-colored cat.

Everyone was here, including several thieves and ladies-in-waiting who hadn't been seen since the book had burned those many years ago. She looked around and was surprised to see Pingree in his jingling green jester's costume, riding on a swayback mule and juggling four oranges.

She nodded at him cautiously.

"Princess!" he called out. "Why did you put on your right shoe first today?"

"My what?"

"You wouldn't want to put on your *wrong* shoe!" he said, and he laughed a squeaky laugh.

"I see," she said, looking at him closely.

"What did the big toe say to the little toe?"

"Are you all right, Pingree?"

"It didn't say anything, silly brains. Toes can't talk!"

She watched as the tired-looking mule carried him past her down the road. Do he know? she thought. Does he remember? Do any of them remember? They all looked the same, but not the same. Their costumes were in unfamiliar styles and brighter colors than before. Her mother was thinner and had a different nose. Her father wore a shorter beard. None of it mattered.

Grandly, King Walther led the way into the castle and took possession. He offered up a prayer of thanks and gave a long speech, which everyone cheered.

But before the first juggler could toss the first ball in the air, a green-tailed bird squawked, "Reader! Reader!" and flapped from the head of a gargoyle. Then a split appeared in the eastern sky, like a torn seam. The breach widened, lifting away the whole blue dome, and suddenly, instead of clouds and birds, an enormous face appeared. A hush settled over the crowd.

"How do you like it?" came a woman's echoey voice.

"What page are we on?" the king whispered urgently to Sylvie. "We've got a Reader!"

But Sylvie stepped out from the crowd and looked up, smiling. "We love it!" she shouted.

"Good!" came the voice above them. "I hope the costumes are okay. You know they had to get a new illustrator."

"Oh, they're wonderful!"

"Sylvie!" hissed the queen. "What are you *doing?*"

"Don't worry, Mother. This isn't an ordinary Reader. Listen, everyone! I'd like you to meet the Writer!"

A gasp swept over the crowd. "The Writer!" they whispered, one to another.

"It's the Writer!"

"Who did she say?"

Many fell to their knees.

The king removed his crown and bowed his head. The queen curtsied deeply.

"For these our many blessings, we thank thee, O great Writer," intoned the king.

"You're quite welcome!" said Lily. "Well, I don't want to stop you from getting settled in. I'll look in on you later. A lot of other people will, too, I think," she said. "I understand the first printing is forty thousand."

The courtiers looked at one another in amazement. Forty thousand Readers?

"Better rest up. I have a feeling you're going to be pretty busy from now on."

The book closed gently, and the backup lights came on immediately, just the right shade of robin's egg blue.

"Nothing like a new book!" exclaimed the king's chief councillor, taking in a deep breath. "Smell those fresh pages!"

"Yes, wonderful, wonderful," the king replied,

but he was chewing on the end of his mustache. "Forty thousand readers! Oh dear."

The celebration continued all afternoon. Princess Sylvie found herself surrounded by well-wishers offering gifts and congratulations. At one point she turned around, still laughing, and found herself looking into the serious eyes of Norbert Fangl.

"Princess?" he said.

"Oh!" She embraced him. "Thank God!"

"I won't ask how you did it," he said.

"No, don't," she said quickly. "You're one of my tutors, if anyone asks."

She looked at his hands, then at his clear forehead and cheek. "You're looking well," she said, smiling so brightly, she almost cried.

"Perfectly well, Your Highness."

She nodded.

"*Thank you,*" he whispered, gripping her hands tightly for a moment, then moving off into the crowd.

Sylvie was immediately surrounded again. She was glad to see everyone, but kept glancing around in odd corners as if she had lost something. Finally, she excused herself and went out for a walk. The Mere of Remind, she discovered, was no longer on page 35 but on page 42, and the illustration was much larger than before. She sat by the cliff and looked out over the water. A blue dragonfly whizzed by.

She had done her best. Everything had turned out wonderfully. She had no right to feel sad.

Just then she noticed a V-shaped ripple in the water, then a little wave as a fin broke the surface. She jumped up. "Fish!" she cried. "Fish!" She ran to the water's edge.

It was her invisible fish, swimming in lazy circles in the Mere. It slid up beside her, its dorsal fin trembling.

"Dear, dear fish!" cried Sylvie and clapped her hands.

Then a miraculous thing happened. The great beast slowly opened its jaws, and out stepped the person Sylvie had been searching for all day.

"Sylvie!" said the girl with the dark blue eyes, arranging the shoulder of her blue cape.

"Oh!" Sylvie cried, jumping up and down and getting her new shoes soaked.

The friends hugged each other.

"You got here!" Sylvie squealed.

The girl gave her a scolding smile. "I know what you did, Princess Sylvie."

"I had to. I had to write you into the book."

"Me and that other fellow."

"Oh, Fangl won't bother anybody."

"You weren't supposed to change a word."

"I know. That's why I wrote you only a small part. Nobody will even notice that the third lady-in-waiting has a new helper."

"The Author will know."

"Oh, that's all right, she doesn't care."

The girl took Sylvie's hand. "I don't mean the Writer. I mean the Author."

"The one who thought all this up in the first place?"

She nodded.

"Oh." Sylvie looked at the wet sand. "But he must have died a long time ago."

"She. And she's very much alive."

"How could that be?"

Her friend looked at her. "Are you alive?"

"Well, I *hope* so!" said Sylvie.

"Well, then?"

Sylvie grew quiet. "Is she very angry?"

The girl threw her a smile.

"Have you spoken with her?" Sylvie persisted.

They started walking along the curve of the shoreline.

"What did she *say?*" said Sylvie. "What does she *look* like?"

"She can look like anything."

"What do you mean?"

"She has more disguises than you could ever guess."

A cricket crawled onto Sylvie's shoe.

"What about him? Is he one of her disguises?"

The girl with the dark blue eyes didn't answer.

"What about the sun?" Sylvie closed her eyes and felt the warmth on her eyelids. "What about the wind?"

The girls continued their walk, jabbering like the best old friends. In the distance, blue and white pennants waved from the castle turrets. A breeze riffled the lake.

All at once a commotion erupted as bullfrogs belched out their warning: "Oooopen! Booook open!" A bright bird exploded out of the underbrush, screaming.

Then the sky opened, and the first new Reader peered down.

Roderick Townley has written ten books of poetry, fiction, nonfiction, and literary criticism. He taught in Chile on a Fulbright fellowship, worked in New York as an editor, and now writes from his home in Kansas. He has two children, Jesse and Grace, and is married to poet Wyatt Townley.